MW00452440

THE ATHLETE-STUDENT:

Freshman Year

Eli,

Keep Pushing,
Hope you enjoy.

EUGENE D. HOLLOMAN

The Athlete-Student: Freshman Year

Copyright © 2018 by Eugene D. Holloman. All rights reserved.

No part of this book may be reproduced or transmitted in any form or by any means, electronic or mechanical, including photocopying, recording, or by any information storage and retrieval system, without the express written permission of the author.

ISBN-13: 978-0-6929792-4-2

Author Email: contact@theathletestudent.com

www.theathletestudent.com

Editor: Lauren Michelle Smith
Interior Design: Lauren Michelle Smith
Cover: Marcus Duenas

TABLE OF CONTENTS

ACKNOWLEDGMENTS

Above all, I want to thank God for choosing me to share this story with the world. I want to thank my wife, Andrea, and my brother, Tim, for supporting me through the book writing process. I want to thank the rest of my family, who supported and encouraged me in spite of all the time it took me away from them.

I would like to express my gratitude to the many people who saw me through this book; to all those who provided support, talked things over, read, wrote, offered comments, and assisted in the editing, proofreading, and design.

I would like to thank the staff of Bayside High, James Madison, and Regent University for their encouragement and development throughout the years.

And last but not least, I beg for forgiveness from all those who have been with me over the years and whose names I've failed to mention.

1 HERO BALL

THERE WERE ONLY TWO MINUTES and forty-five seconds remaining in the fourth quarter. My squad was trailing Monroe High School by four points after their all-state running back broke for a sixty-five-yard touchdown to take the lead. The local newspaper billed it as the game of the century in the weeks leading up. Headlines read: "Can Monroe High Monstrous Defense Contain Bayside's Michael 'Tootie' Mayberry?"

When we received the kickoff, I knew we were going to drive down the field and win the game. We had home-field advantage, and our stadium was packed with the loudest and liveliest crowd I'd ever witnessed. The energy was so electrifying; it felt like the entire stadium was rocking. There was a tremendous sense of school pride as the crowd filled the stands, donning our school's colors of red and gold.

Twenty yards down and eighty to go with two minutes and forty seconds to spare is more than enough time left on the clock to score the winning touchdown. I received the handoff and sprinted through the defense for a twelve-yard gain. I could hear the student section shouting, "TOOTIE! TOOTIE!" It was as if everyone in the stadium knew who was going to win this game for us. During the next play, I received a pitch to the right, only to be greeted by two enormous, hulk-looking defensive linemen in dark green jerseys. Within seconds, I eluded the first tackler's attempt to take me down. The second defender was no better as I juked him right out of his shoes for another twenty-yard gain. The next three plays stalled as the clock read thirty-six seconds.

"Time out!" Coach Perkins yelled.

As we huddled on the sideline, I told Coach to get me the ball. He looked down at his sheet and called a play intended for me.

I was born to compete, and I was built for moments like this, were the only thoughts that consumed my mind. Some called it selfishness, but I believed in reaping the rewards of pumping iron throughout the year and running sprints in the oppressive heat—all for the sweet glory of winning. So excuse me for being a bit cocky.

Confident is more like it, as we ran onto the field and lined up. Three wide receivers stood on the opposite side. I guess that's why so many college scouts had been lining up outside of Coach Perkins' office, searching for the next game-changing athlete. At six feet, two hundred and five pounds—with a sub 4.3 forty-yard dash—I was what you'd call a major university's dream come true. From running back to linebacker, I could do it all.

At the hike of the football, I took off, using every millisecond of what my forty-yard dash time suggested. With a glance over my shoulder, the ball spiraled and landed beautifully in my hands. With one man to beat, the defensive back instantly squared me up to anticipate my next move. I planted my left foot in the dirt to assist my change in direction to the right. As the defender lunged forward, thinking he had my move figured out, I quickly jittered both feet before stopping in my tracks as he landed on his face. It was the nastiest shake and bake move I'd performed to date and would most likely become a centerpiece of my highlight film. I skipped into the end zone as the clock ticked zero. In pandemonium fashion, teammates and fans rushed me, screaming, "TOOTIE! TOOTIE! TOOTIE!" It was single-handedly the best moment of my life. We defeated our arch rivals by two points.

Minutes after celebrating, I waded through the sea of people and headed toward the locker room.

"Good game, handsome," I heard from a familiar, beautiful voice.

I gave Sophia a hug and a kiss. She and I had been dating since the ninth grade, and she remained an inspirational figure in my life. She was top of our senior class with a 4.0 GPA and got accepted into every school she applied to. Not only was she smart, she was the finest girl I'd ever laid eyes on. The first moment I saw her, it was my goal to make her mine.

"Thank you, beautiful."

"I see you used those moves I taught you out there on the field," she joked, having the most contagious laugh and beautiful smile.

4

"Something like that."

As a local reporter began to swarm me for a post-game interview, Sophia and I departed each other's company.

"Tootie, you left nothing to be desired out there, how were you able to rack up 215 total yards against that juggernaut Monroe defense?" the reporter asked.

I paused for a minute to gather my thoughts because, in my head, I thought I should've had 350 yards. However, I decided against stating my disappointment, as one unfavorable answer could start an uproar.

"You have to give those guys credit, they are a well-deserving team, but our coach put together a masterful game plan and we executed," I replied.

After a few more questions, I headed back to the locker room, only to get stopped by Coach Perkins.

"The coach from the University of Virginia is waiting for you to commit, son. I think it will be a great fit for you."

"I don't know, Coach P," I replied as I walked off.

We just won the biggest game in school history and he has the nerve to ask me about choosing a college? How about good game, or I'm proud of you.

Coach Perkins had been pushing me to attend the University of Virginia (UVA) for a while now. He regularly preached academics and the opportunity to become the first college graduate in my family. But nowhere in Coach Perkins' nudging did he ever mention me being a college football star. For four years now, he'd asked me to write down goals before the beginning of each season, and every year I wrote about being a star football player and playing professionally. Oftentimes, I wondered what big picture Coach P was envisioning for me. I wondered if he even considered my goals.

But he was right about one thing: I needed to make a decision on where I'd be playing next fall, and the two years after. I say that because as soon as I could put my name in the NFL draft, I would. I had everything all mapped out. I was going to kill it in college and become a first-round draft pick, then go on to have a Hall of Fame football career. To be honest, the education aspect was the least of my worries. Even though Sophia constantly talked about different areas of study, I had no clue what a major was and didn't care.

She would say things like, "I'm going to major in prelaw. You should major in business or economics, and once we graduate, we can start our own line of businesses."

That was Sophia, always planning ahead and thinking about our future. But all I could think about was putting myself on the map and getting drafted to the league.

2 GROWING UP

I WAS GIVEN THE NAME Tootie by my dad, Reggie, because I was the smallest and youngest out of his two sons. According to him, as a toddler, I would always compete against my brother every chance I got. While I was often on the losing end, I never backed down. Sometimes I won based on my talent, or he got tired of me hounding him and decided to let me win. Either way, the determination I displayed inspired the nickname.

My mother passed away from cancer when I was two years old. I don't remember much about her, but my dad has a knack for telling fascinating stories that capture her beauty. According to him, my mother would attend local jazz concerts because she loved how the instruments would blend, formulating smooth melodies. One of the most memorable stories was when he and my mother were out listening to a local jazz band. The pianist rushed off the stage to tend to an emergency, leaving the group clueless as to what had occurred. After a couple minutes, the lead musician asked the crowd if anyone knew how to play Etta James' "At Last" on the piano. Without any hesitation, my mother jumped on stage and filled in for the missing pianist, just as if she were a member of the band.

Every time my dad tells this story, he becomes very animated and finishes by saying, "Your mother didn't miss a beat, either."

My dad was a pipe layer for the city of Virginia Beach for twenty years and often worked late shifts—not only to make ends meet, but to provide my brother and me with the things he didn't have growing up. Out of all my friends, he was the only dad I knew of who was around and involved in his children's lives. I always thought of him as a superhero for raising us on his own.

Despite working late, Dad never missed any of my football games. He never criticized any of my coaches or belittled any referees. Instead, he left all his criticism for me. After every game, he would point out the negatives, even if I thought I played flawlessly. "You looked timid out there today, son." Or he would say something along the lines of, "How are you going to be better than Emmitt Smith performing like that?" At times his criticism seemed like verbal assaults, but he knew how to light a fire under me so I would always feel as if I had something to prove. While others told me I was great, a superstar, or the best thing to come out of Virginia Beach, I remained motivated and humbled by the lack of praise my dad gave.

Truth be told, I wasn't sure of the impact my mother's death had had on him. The stories he shared of her lacked a certain emotion. We were raised to be hard; showing sadness was considered a weakness in the Mayberry household. I remember getting upset when classmates teased me for not having a mother.

"What's wrong?" my dad had asked, after seeing me in tears after a long bus ride home one afternoon.

"Some of the kids in my class teased me about being the only one without a mom."

"You have to toughen up, son. Forget what others have to say."

And just like that, at six years old, I began to suppress how I felt. I mastered the old saying, *"Never let them see you sweat"* by giving stoic impressions.

My father was also a ladies' man. Every week there seemed to be a different woman coming over to the house. I guess his heart had remained closed. Perhaps that was his way of dealing with the loss of my mother. I was always afraid of adopting the same lifestyle. I never knew what a healthy marriage looked like outside of watching sitcoms on television, but one thing I was sure of: I was going to marry Sophia.

Mom's death took the biggest toll on my older brother, Shawn, who was eight at the time of her passing. Unbeknownst to Dad, Shawn began to follow the wrong crowd by the time he reached middle school. I vividly re-member the heavy aroma of marijuana on his clothes after he would get me off the bus on the days Dad worked late. Although Shawn ran with the local wannabe thugs, he was very smart. He never had to study to ace an exam. In fact, Shawn was my role model. Slightly more handsome, but far less athletic than me; if you could name it, Shawn was good at it. It just so happened that some of the things he was good at turned out to be to his downfall. Shooting dice, selling weed, and slanging stolen merchandise were just a few ways Shawn mastered the art of hustling. Still, he protected me in a way only an older brother could. He would never let me hang with his friends, and if I thought about drinking or smoking, my face would be introduced to his fist repeatedly.

Life as we knew it began to unravel during the summer leading up to my middle school arrival. I was twelve, and Shawn was an eighteen-year-old rising senior at Bayside High. After years of concealing the drug use and illegal cash flow, a Virginia Beach police detective called my father to inform him that Shawn had been booked on aggravated malicious wounding and possession of firearm charges.

"WHAT?!" my dad screamed, as the look of devastation seeped into his eyes. His shoulders slumped. "You know what, Officer? If my boy did what he was accused of, he deserves to be in there with the rest of them crimi-nals."

After my dad had hung up with the detective, he asked me if I ever saw my brother doing anything he wasn't sup-posed to be doing.

"No sir," I replied.

That was the first time I could remember telling my dad a lie. No matter what I saw Shawn doing, I could never snitch on him—even to my dad.

Dad came closer and said in a soft tone, "I've always asked you boys what it is you want to be when you grow up. I ask that because I believe you can do anything, and I mean *anything*, but not once have I ever heard the word *thug* or *criminal* come out of your mouths."

He walked off, and after hearing of Shawn's incarcer-ation and seeing the utter disappointment from his face, I felt as if the walls were closing in. *Maybe I should've said something.* Losing my brother to prison made the idea of not trying to stop it beforehand seem foolish.

During the months leading up to Shawn's trial, my dad refused to accept his calls from jail, and he never hired an attorney to represent him. I wasn't sure if Dad was showing tough love, or pulling away from his oldest child because of the perceived betrayal. Either way, Shawn was forced to use a court-appointed attorney. The day before his trial, he called collect and I anxiously accepted it.

"What's up, bro?" Shawn asked in a raspy tone.

"Nothing much, how are you holding up?" I inquired.

"The jail be recording these conversations, so don't ask me nothing about the case, but other than having ten years over my head and eating trash every day, I'm holding up fine," he said firmly. "How are you doing? How's Dad?"

"I'm doing okay. It's hard not having you here, though. Everything is so different now, and Dad hasn't really said much."

"Yeah, I figured. I will say this, though, I'm not guilty of what they're trying to pin on me."

"I know, Shawn, I know."

"No matter what happens tomorrow, know that you have a gift from God, lil' bro. You can take this football thing to the limit. Keep a straight head, and go and get it."

15

We talked for several minutes and after the call ended, I prayed to God, asking him not to take my brother away from me.

The next day at nine in the morning, I attended the court hearing with one of my aunties. My dad didn't want to come. Even at twelve years old, I felt like if I ever messed up and landed in the same situation as my brother, my dad would turn his back on me, too. The thought of appeasing him with perfection almost put more pressure on me than I'd put on myself.

Shawn's hearing was my first experience inside of a courtroom, and hopefully my last. I still remember when his accuser took the stand and gave his testimony:

"Me and the gentleman sitting across from me, known as Shawn Mayberry, were playing a game of dice when an argument ensued over winnings. He was enraged about losing, and he attacked me, using a nine-millimeter gun. He bashed me across the head repeatedly until the altercation was broken up by bystanders."

I wanted to scream, "Nah, he's lying. My brother wouldn't do nothing like that!"

The prosecutors recommended ten years of jail time for my brother. After being presented with the evidence and a short deliberation, the judge began announcing her verdict. I could feel my body harden like a block of concrete. She said to Shawn, "The court sentences you to ten years in the custody of the Virginia Department of Corrections. The court reduces the sentence by four years; thus, making your sentence six years in the custody of Virginia Department of Corrections."

At the time I didn't fully understand the magnitude of those words, but I knew it was bad when my auntie dropped her head in defeat. Immediately after, I saw Shawn drop his head into his chest and take deep breaths, as if he were crying.

Shortly thereafter, the bailiff escorted him out of the courtroom. As he was walking out—shackles on his wrists and ankles—he subtly lifted his head and made eye contact with me. Then he pounded his chest twice—a gesture I took to mean "stay strong." But that meant nothing as I cried my eyes out, realizing my best friend would be gone for the next six years.

3 RECRUIT ME

SWEAT WAS DRIPPING FROM MY hands and I had butterflies in my stomach the size of golf balls. Like most soon-to-be college students, the SAT was a big deal, but even more so for me as I only had a 2.32 GPA. Per the requirements, I needed to score at least an 890 on the test to become college eligible. Looking across the room, I compared myself to all the smarter-looking students. *Why do I have to take this dumb test anyway? I'm just trying to play ball, not become a doctor or scientist.* The only reason I didn't run out of the classroom before the test had started was because of the encouragement I'd received from Sophia, who took the test her junior year and scored 1570. She tried her best to prep me, but there was no preparation for sitting in the room literally seconds before taking a test that would determine if I could pursue my lifelong dream.

"You may start," the administrator announced.

I took one gigantic gasp of air as if it was going to be my last breath on earth and began answering questions from the reading section. Immediately, I wished I would've taken my high school English courses a little more seriously. I remembered bits and pieces of what I was taught, but I could only imagine where I'd be if I'd applied myself by giving a solid effort to really learn.

For sixty-five minutes, I read through passages before moving on to the math and writing sections. The entire test took roughly three hours to complete. As I walked out of the classroom, I felt those golf balls in my stomach transform into bowling balls. I was even more anxious to find out my score.

I raced to my car and called Sophia.

"How did it go?" she asked.

"I think it went well," I replied, sounding unsure.

"I know you did well."

"Thanks for always being there for me. I don't know where I would be if it weren't for you."

"You're welcome. Once you get your scores back, we'll have to celebrate."

"How long does it take for the results to come back, anyway? I have an official visit with the University of Georgia next weekend, and I would rather not answer all those questions about qualifying."

"I think it took me about three weeks to get my SAT results back," Sophia answered. "But I didn't think you were considering Georgia, so why are you taking a visit there?"

"Come on, I thought we talked about this."

"We sure didn't. I would've remembered."

"Well, looking at their roster, and from what the coaches have told me, I could come in and start as a true freshman for a perennial powerhouse program."

"Ohhhhhh, okaaaaaaay," Sophia said.

Sophia wanted us to go to the same college or stay closer together, as she was considering staying closer to home. She narrowed her choices to William & Mary, University of Richmond, or James Madison University. All terrific schools, but lacking the big, national, headline-grabbing football programs that could help me become a future first-round draft pick.

"It's not all about football, baby," she said. "God forbid, what if you get hurt? Then what? Why not pick a school that has both—a good football program closer to home, but can also guarantee you a good education? Like, how are we going to even see each other?"

"Well, I have to go to class no matter where I decide to go, but my path is clear. Enrolling in a smaller or losing program will only to derail me from my goal."

"So, you would actually go miles away and leave me?" she asked.

Not really knowing how to respond, I went with, "No matter where I go to college, it will be for a limited amount of time, and we will be right back side by side before you know it."

As I arrived home, I saw an unfamiliar car in our driveway, which was quickly dismissed as one of my dad's girlfriend's. Shockingly enough, it was the University of Virginia's head football coach, Mike Ford. He was sitting on the couch across from my dad and Coach Perkins when I walked in.

"How are you doing, son?" Coach Ford greeted. "I know you had a chance to meet all the other coaches on my staff, but I wanted to surprise you and introduce myself personally."

"I'm doing well, and nice to meet you, Coach."

"Do you like to be called Michael, Mike, or Tootie?" he asked.

"I don't have a preference."

"Tootie it is then! What an awesome nickname, by the way," he said with a grin. "How do you think you did on your test this morning?"

"I'm sure I got the score I needed to qualify."

"Great, well I know you've been pondering our offer to become the next great Virginia Cavalier, but I also want you to know once you are a Cavalier, you're a Cavalier for life. We not only want to win games, we want to win at life. My job is to coach you *off* the field, as well as on."

"That's all we could ask for," my dad chimed in.

"I've been telling Tootie this is what he should look for in a college," Coach Perkins added.

"I appreciate your transparency, Coach. For as long as I can remember, I've wanted to be a professional football player; I can't see myself doing anything else. I believe I was born to play in college, and then professionally. A good education is great, but what about helping me become the next Tiki Barber?" I asked.

"I've sat in countless living rooms and always shoot it straight. The reality is that there are over four hundred and fifty thousand student-athletes, and only a handful go on to play professionally. I would be doing you a disservice if I promised you that you were going to go pro after a couple of years. I thought I was going to play professionally, too, but it didn't happen. Not because I wasn't good enough, but because luck wasn't on my side. One thing I did do was get was a degree in communications that no knee injury or ruptured Achilles could ever take away from me."

"Yes, sir," I replied, even though I still wasn't sold. However, my dad and Coach P were. Unfortunately, Coach Ford wasn't able to promote winning seasons, or even a history of successful professional players under his tenure. His program was not consistently winning national championships—or conference championships, for that matter. Last year his team only won three games and sent zero players into the league. So, his only play was to sell me on getting an education.

As the conversation continued, Coach Ford repositioned himself on the leather couch and leaned toward me. "Tootie, football aside, what do you see yourself doing with your life?"

The question was all too familiar, and one my dad and Sophia had asked me a million times. *Why do I have to choose a plan B? Why is it frowned upon to have only one plan and work relentlessly to achieve it? I have decided long ago football is my only plan, and if it doesn't work out, I will choose something else.*

"Coach, football is my life," I explained.

Once those words left my mouth, it felt like I had suffocated the room. I was pretty sure I was going to get an earful from my dad and Coach P afterward.

"You are a pretty stern seventeen-year-old. I admire that. Look, we have you as a top priority in our recruiting class this year, and I would like to know now before February's signing date—which is two-and-a-half months away—if you would commit to becoming a Cavalier?" Coach Ford said.

"I have an official visit with the University of Georgia next weekend, so I want to wait until closer to signing day before I make my decision," I responded.

He promptly sat back on the couch. "I've heard rumblings about your upcoming visit. I know they are a top ten ball club and probably offering you everything under the sun, but don't discount all we have to offer. I can't give you the glitz and glamour, but I can take care of you like you are my son. I expect to hear back soon, regardless of where you decide to go."

Coach Ford didn't make it out of the driveway before the lecturing began. My dad never went to college, so his thoughts were for me to get drafted and play professionally, but also major in something lucrative in case football didn't pan out. Coach Perkins, on the other hand, had seen athletes from the area get exploited by their talents and tossed to the side by coaches as soon as eligibility expired or performance was not what they were expecting. They both seemed to like how family-oriented Coach Ford was, but I wasn't going to let any university exploit me. Every college had their sales pitch, and it was hard to determine which was sincere, so I figured I would be candid about my goals and attend a university that could help me obtain them.

4 COMMITTED

RECRUITING VISITS ARE LIKE AN all-expense-paid vacation with the hopes of the university acquiring your services—at least, that's how I saw it. I knew I was in for an epic weekend when my father and I flew first class into Athens, Georgia. I instantly dismissed the horror stories I'd heard about flying, like the waiting hours in the terminal before boarding, fighting over overhead space, getting served small, salty bags of peanuts, listening to the screams of crying babies, dealing with snoring from the overweight guy beside you, and losing your belongings. But, what I experienced was surreal. I stretched out in the most comfortable seat ever while watching a movie and eating everything from fresh fruit, to an ice cream sundae. *A guy could certainly get used to this.*

Upon our arrival, we were greeted by the University of Georgia's offensive coordinator, Wes Smith, and their All-American junior quarterback, Terrell Knight.

"You must be Tootie Mayberry," Coach Smith said, extending his right hand. "How was the flight in?"

I shook his hand while making direct eye contact. "That was the best plane ride of my life! Well, that was my first plane ride ever, but still.... I can already tell you guys know how to do it here."

"Tootie, we are first class, there's no other way to explain it," Coach Smith said. "Meet Terrell. He will be your host this weekend. He'll show you what being a student-athlete at the University of Georgia is all about."

My dad and I introduced ourselves to Terrell and jumped into Coach Smith's Cadillac Escalade. Jay-Z lyrics flowed through his speakers, grabbing my attention.

"Hold up, do you really listen to hip-hop, or are you fooling me right now?" I asked.

Coach Smith turned the volume up a little higher as he looked back at me. "When you have over ninety-five players who you consider your children, their interests naturally become yours."

Our first stop was at the University of Georgia's football stadium, better known as Sanford Stadium. The weather was in the low sixties, but as soon as I exited the car, the goose bumps that took over my body made the temperature feel like it was a frigid twenty degrees. We walked directly into the stadium and onto the oval G at the fifty-yard line.

"Look around and envision yourself playing in front of ninety thousand screaming fans," Coach Smith said.

As soon as I began to take it all in, I was interrupted by the massive scoreboard. "Now starting at tailback, standing at six feet and weighing two hundred and twenty-five pounds, from Virginia Beach, Virginia, number seven, Michael Tootie Mayyyyyyyberry!" the PA announcer yelled. I stood in awe as the scoreboard showed some of my high school highlights.

Noticeably quiet, my dad leaned in and whispered, "Don't get distracted by all of this, son." I knew it was coming; it was just a matter of time before he felt the need to yank me back to reality. He must have read my mind. I brushed off his comments.

You deserve this treatment, Tootie, take it all in.

After the mid-field presentation, Terrell gave us a tour of the football facilities—starting with the locker room. I'd been on other college visits, but nothing compared to this locker room. Inside of each locker was the name of the athlete who wore the same jersey number in prior years. One day in the near future, a recruit was going to stand here and say, "Wow! Tootie Mayberry wore this jersey number. I have big shoes to fill." Just the thought gave me chills.

The equipment room was just as impressive. The staff let me pick out as much gear as I could carry. I made sure to grab Sophia a t-shirt in hopes of making it up to her when I got back home.

After the tour, we ate lunch and checked into a five-star hotel close to campus. Terrell mentioned he was coming back later to pick me up and show me what college nightlife was like. After the incident with Shawn, my father did not have a long leash on me. I was always in the house by 11:00 p.m., except for the times I stayed overnight at my auntie's house, who gave me a little more freedom. Even with the added freedom, I didn't abuse it by staying out late partying. If anything, Sophia and I would catch a late-night movie.

My dad put down his luggage and took a deep breath. "You are becoming a man, son. I never stepped foot on a college campus until your recruitment process started, and now that I have, it makes me wish I would've taken advantage of the opportunities I had. You say you want to play professional ball, right?"

"Yes, sir," I responded.

"Then every decision you make here on out will dictate your path."

I knew what my dad was getting at, even if he didn't want to say it. He'd done everything in his power to keep me from making the same mistakes as my brother. He knew he had to remove the shelter he provided and let me be a man.

After showering, I decided on wearing a Georgia hoodie I'd received from the equipment staff. I hopped into the car with Terrell and was eager to see what college life was like in Georgia.

"Coach mentioned that you have the potential to start as a freshman. I do think we are one playmaker away at the running back position from competing for a national championship," Terrell said.

"My goal is to come right in and make an immediate impact. That's what you did and look, you are about to be a first-round selection next year."

Terrell looked at me intently and smirked. "Everything is not as it always seems."

"What do you mean by that?" I asked.

"Never mind, let's go in and get this night started," he replied.

We walked into a semi-dirty apartment with a group of football players and a couple of females scattered throughout. Some were watching television. Some were on their phones having causal conversations, while others were playing a game that involved throwing a ping pong ball into red cups.

"This is Tootie, he's a running back from Virginia," Terrell said loudly over the chatter.

"What's up?" they all said collectively.

34

Before I could reply, a stocky dude sitting in the far corner yelled, "So, you are the guy who is going to be my understudy for the next two years."

Laughter ensued.

I wanted to say, "I bet you couldn't even hold my jock strap," or better yet, "You must not know the cloth I'm cut from to say something as foolish as that," but thought better of it. I'd yet to get a feel for my environment, and I didn't want to start any beef.

"If you have something to teach me, I would be more than happy to learn," I responded.

That seemed to do the trick.

"Do you want something to drink, Tootie?" Terrell asked.

I wasn't sure what he was offering, but by the looks of the bottles on the kitchen counter, I assumed he meant liquor.

"No, thanks, I'm good."

"Come on, Virginia, it's tradition that we take a shot with recruits," the stocky guy who addressed me earlier pressed. I learned his name was Dominque Jones. He was a junior who rarely played after being a sought-after recruit coming out of high school.

"You know my name is not Virginia," I said.

"Dude, you gotta lighten up," he responded, handing me a shot glass filled with vodka.

Normally I didn't fall for peer pressure, but I wasn't sure how it was going to play out with the rest of the guys if I declined to take the shot. I took it without hesitation; the vodka burned the back of my throat.

"Hold up, rookie, we have to take the shot together as a unit," one of the upperclassmen said.

They handed me another one and everyone yelled "salud," then proceeded to hammer it down. I followed suit with the hopes of gaining their respect.

Alcohol was never my thing. I tried it once my junior year after a playoff victory, but the taste left much to be desired. Normally when I declined offers, there was never any pushback. I knew from other recruiting visits that drinking was the thing to do for college students, but up until now, I'd always avoided the pitfall. Suddenly, the idea of seeing a future first-round pick consume alcohol made it not seem like the worst thing in the world.

We all left the house to attend a nearby party. As we were walking, I started to feel the alcohol's effects. My vision was blurry, and everything around me was moving at a slower pace. When we arrived, every person turned their attention to Terrell. Some even took out their phones to snap photos and ask for autographs. A small part of me became envious. I couldn't wait to become the big man on campus and receive the same admiration.

Two beautiful, young ladies approached Terrell to ask for a selfie, to which he agreed. Afterwards, he introduced the young ladies to me.

"This is Tootie. We're hoping he comes here next year to help us win a championship."

"Tootie? That name is as cute as you are," one of the beauties said. "Why wouldn't you want to come here and play alongside Terrell and help us win?"

Staring deeply into her eyes, I found myself so mesmerized that I almost forgot about Sophia. I shook my head and regained focus. "We'll see."

My mind continued to race as I found a quiet spot in the corner. I didn't understand all that was going on around me, but I knew I'd lost focus on two different

occasions. First, it was the vodka. Then it was noticing the good looks of someone who wasn't my girlfriend. It may have seemed like two small instances, but I secretly wanted more. I wanted to lose focus and enjoy the night and worry about the consequences later.

It was 12:00 a.m. when I asked Terrell to take me back to the hotel.

"You ready to go back already?" he asked.

"Yeah, I'm getting tired, plus I have to meet with Coach Stuart in the morning."

Coach Stuart was the head coach of the University of Georgia football team, and the last thing I wanted to do was show any signs of weariness from a long night of partying.

Terrell agreed to take me back to the hotel, and on our way, he said, "It's a lot to take in, huh? The partying, the drinking, the girls, and you haven't seen the football or school side of things yet. There's no way to prepare for it, either. When you decide to come here and start scoring touchdowns, your life will change. They say stay humble, but what does that look like? The good thing is you have resources all around you."

I soaked up everything he was saying. I was still convinced that I could handle anything that came my way, but now I had a better understanding of what stardom looked like.

At breakfast the next morning, I gulped down some of the best French toast that my taste buds had ever experienced while Coach Stuart talked about the future of the program. He gave a similar sales pitch as other coaches, you know, the family atmosphere and how he looks after each athlete like they were his children. But his vibe was different—more like overly confident with a splash of arrogance. He wanted me to come to Georgia, but his stance was that his program was going to win with or without me. Total reverse psychology. Still, he was a coach I could see myself playing for. He was the first coach I'd talked to that didn't make me feel entitled, and if I chose the University of Georgia, everything I'd receive would have to be earned.

5 NATIONAL SIGNING DAY

"I DON'T KNOW WHAT'S GOTTEN into you lately; you are changing," Sophia said angrily. "You used to talk to me about everything, and now you barely speak more than two words."

"What are you talking about? I just have a lot on my plate and a lot going through my mind, I don't even know how to make sense of everything right now," I replied.

"You can't even tell me what college you are going to choose. You act like I wasn't the one staying up late with you helping you get a 975 on the SAT, or being your biggest cheerleader at each of your games," she said, seemingly confused.

"It's not that, Sophia. Trust me. Shawn just came home last month from doing six years in prison, and now thirty days later, I have to make a huge decision on where

I'm going to school. Do I stay close to you and my family? Do I go to another state and leave behind the stress and pressure everyone is putting on me? I wish I had some peace, but I don't know."

National Signing Day was the biggest and most joyous day for athletes. Recruitment was over, and the next step was signing a scholarship to join whichever school you felt you would benefit from the most. For years I followed where each athlete from our area had chosen to play. In the media, it always looked like a celebration, but for me, it'd become a nightmare.

Shawn moved back into my father's house after his release, so tensions were running high. The relationship needed work. Heck, they hadn't even discussed the incident. It was weird to be around, and I was sure I wasn't the only noticing the elephant in the room.

Over the past two months since my visit to Georgia, I'd visited Virginia Tech, University of Miami, University of Virginia, and Ohio State University. All terrific schools with a history of getting players drafted into the NFL. Still, I wasn't sure what college I'd choose at tomorrow's press conference.

It didn't matter where I was at, people always came up to me and asked, "Where are you going to school?" Everyone from teachers, to coaches, to students, to friends and family…even strangers. It'd gotten to the point where I couldn't recognize people's intentions, including my family's. It used to be all about me as a person, and now it was about me as a football player. I was partly to blame. I'd made my dreams known to everyone who would listen, and now my dream had become theirs.

My dad took me out for dinner to my favorite Italian restaurant to help clear my mind a bit. In the weeks leading up to National Signing Day, he only gave his opinion on each school I visited if I asked for it. He wanted me to take the initiative in gathering all the facts from each one and make my own decision based on my gut feeling. At this very moment, part of me wished he was like the dominant parents who made some of the hard choices for their children.

I could barely eat my alfredo as I twirled the noodles back in forth in my bowl, thinking about the pros and cons of each university. At the University of Virginia, I could instantly become the man and stay close to Sophia, Shawn, and my dad. The University of Georgia would allow me to be a freshman starter for a national powerhouse, and the University of Miami was known for putting players into the league. I wasn't quite feeling Virginia Tech and Ohio State University as much as the others, so that helped the process along a little bit.

"Tootie, you haven't said a word since we got to the restaurant," my dad said.

"There's really not much to say," I replied.

"Well, talk to me about what you're thinking."

"I mean, there's a lot. Shawn is home, and you guys have not said much of anything to each other. How am I supposed to make a decision seeing our family like this? Then I have Sophia, and you know how I feel about her…. It's just too much."

"I've created some stubborn boys. I know that because I'm more stubborn than the both of you combined. Shawn and I will be okay. What Tootie needs to do is worry about Tootie. Make a decision based on what you want to do. You're sitting here with your face down, but you're going to college, son. The majority of the knuckleheads walking around this neighborhood would love to be in your shoes. Heck, I would love to be in your shoes, so I suggest you make a decision and stop acting as if it's life or death. There's no wrong choice here, do what your heart is telling you."

As I considered my dad's perspective, the massive weight I'd been carrying on my shoulders lifted. I was leaning toward one particular school. If I still felt the same in the morning, then I'd know what choice to make.

"Today's the day!" I said to myself as I woke from a restless night of tossing and turning.

I dressed in a suit and tie—a must for occasions like today. All eyes would be on me as I stunned the crowd by whatever decision I made.

When I walked into the kitchen for breakfast and saw Shawn and Dad talking it out, I just knew today was going to be special.

"So, what's it going to be?" Shawn asked.

"You'll have to wait just like everybody else," I responded.

When I arrived at school, I headed for the courtyard. Sophia and I had met there every day before first period since we were freshmen. It was where I first asked her to be my girlfriend, and it became our spot afterwards. After waiting for several minutes, my initial thoughts on Sophia's running late quickly turned into *she's not coming*. I called her phone, but no answer.

I'm not going to let this ruin my day. I have to stay composed.

I hurried to my first class, but Coach Perkins stopped me along the way.

"Come into my office, Tootie," he demanded.

"I'm going to be late to class," I complained, already anticipating what he wanted to speak about.

"All of a sudden you care about not being late," he said sarcastically. "Coach Ford has been calling every hour asking me if the University of Virginia is where you intend to play college football this fall. I told him you were keeping a tight lid on your decision, but I want to know, have you decided yet? If you have made a decision, your secret will remain safe with me."

"With all due respect, Coach, I haven't even told my father where I'm going, and I would like to keep it like that until the press conference," I explained.

"I understand, Tootie. Just keep in mind what I said. Your education is the important thing to consider, not just the football program."

"Yes, sir," I responded, before walking to English class.

The day was dragging at a snail's pace. I was physically present, but my mind was elsewhere. All I could think about was this afternoon's press conference. I planned to set three hats on the table. One for the University of Virginia, one for University of Miami, and one for the University of Georgia. I'd announce my intentions by putting on the hat of my preferred school. *I'm sure the crowd will give a standing ovation mixed with screams of joy and flashes from their camera phones.*

Once the crowd settled down, I'd then give a reason of why I chose that school. Maybe I'd say something like, "This university will provide me with the opportunity of fulfilling my lifelong dream of playing college football and continuing my education." But more importantly, after

the press conference was over, I could put this college selection process in my rearview mirror and look forward to
wherever the next steps led.

I made my way down to the auditorium, roughly thirty
minutes before the press conference started. There were
already local and national media members, along with
their camera crews and some of the school staff—including our principal. The auditorium was beautifully deco-
rated with tons of balloons and a cake on the stage that
read: *Congratulations, Tootie.*

"Attention, if you would like to attend Tootie Mayberry's press conference, please make your way quietly to
the auditorium," a voice said over the loudspeaker.

As waves of students and teachers started entering, I
took my seat on stage next to Shawn and Dad. Family
members and teammates sat closer to the stage, while the
student body filled in behind. I caught the eye of Sophia
as she walked in. Strangely enough, it appeared as though
she wanted to enter unnoticed. I quickly dismissed it and
regained focus before reaching into my backpack to grab
the three hats.

Coach Perkins grabbed the microphone to thank and welcome everyone.

"Tootie Mayberry approached me four years ago as a 5'7", 160-pound freshman with enough swagger and confidence to instantly make me believe he was good enough to be our team's water boy. No, all jokes aside, even with his small stature back then, he believed he was going to be the best player to ever grace these hallways. And with a work ethic to back it up, I can say he has achieved his lofty goals. The young man sitting on this stage has represented Bayside High School with integrity throughout his four years here. I believe he can do anything he sets his mind to, and I can't wait for him to reveal his future plans. So, Tootie, there is nothing else to be said. I'll turn the microphone over to you and let you announce the university who will get an outstanding football player, but an even better person."

I could feel the moisture building up from my sweaty armpits as I quickly gathered my thoughts. As I reached across the table to accept the microphone, I said, "First of all, I would like to thank everyone for coming out today, your presence as I make this huge decision is much appreciated. I would like to thank my mother, who is watching from above, and to my dad, Reggie, and my older brother, Shawn. Thank you, guys—so much. I would not be where I am if it weren't for you. Thank you both for helping shape the man I'm growing into. I would like to thank my beautiful girlfriend, Sophia. And last but not least, a big thank you to every teacher, teammate, and student at Bayside High. Now, without further ado, I will be taking my talents and signing with the University of…."

6 OFF I GO

ON THE MORNING I WAS set to leave for training camp, I lay in my bed and reminisced about the last couple of months since I signed my scholarship to play for the University of Georgia. I mostly thought about the aftermath of my college announcement, and the effect it'd had on some of my relationships.

First, there was Coach Perkins. He didn't hesitate in voicing his displeasure. Being that I was the highest ever rated recruit to come out of Bayside High, he thought I set the wrong example for younger athletes by leaving the state. During one of our conversations, he'd said, "The state of Virginia could easily be better known than Florida, Texas, and any other traditional football state if our talent stayed home instead of deciding to go elsewhere to play college ball."

He never gave a reason why Virginia's football popularity mattered, but I'm sure head coaches all over the state persuaded him on the importance of keeping kids home. If I had to guess, that was the reason why he and Coach Ford were always in regular communication with each other.

My disappointment with Coach Perkins stemmed from the fact he preached education to me regularly. Let him tell it, the University of Virginia was so much better than every other college. I would've respected him more if he'd honestly expressed his reasoning behind wanting me to stay home, instead of using the lack of scholars in my family's history to persuade me to choose the University of Virginia.

As far as Sophia's and my relationship, she has since apologized for intentionally avoiding me on National Signing Day, citing selfishness as the reason for steering clear. Her thoughts at the time were to allow me to make a decision based on my dreams, and not using our relationship to influence me to do what she wanted me to do, which was to stay closer to home. I apologized to her as well. I reiterated how important she was in my life and promised not to shut her out if things got difficult again. Sophia chose James Madison University, which was seven hours away from the University of Georgia. She eventually got over the thought of being miles apart, and we both decided to make the long-distance relationship work.

I switched to even happier thoughts, prom and how epic that night was. I burst into laughter when I thought about dropping the corsage after seeing how fine Sophia looked. She wore this gorgeous purple dress with a split to her thigh. It almost made me change my mind about going to Georgia. We were named prom queen and king, and got the opportunity to be center stage, sharing the ceremonial first dance as the DJ played "Love" by Musiq Soulchild.

Time had flown by much faster than I'd anticipated. I wasn't second-guessing my decision, but this was the first instance where I'd be away from Virginia for an extended period of time. Anybody who knew me was aware that I sometimes came off as arrogant, but the fear of the unknown was playing tricks on my mind and confidence. *I foresee myself as being one of the greatest players ever, but what if I get there and don't meet my expectations? What if I get homesick, or something terrible happens to a family member?* All of these different scenarios plagued my mind.

Dad, Shawn, and I decided to leave a day early, being that the drive to Athens was more than 8 hours away. Dad wouldn't let me take my vehicle to school my first year. He'd said he'd heard too many stories of college kids' involvement in alcohol-related accidents. I was initially bummed, but those were his rules.

As we pulled out of our driveway to begin our journey, Shawn looked back at me from the passenger seat and said, "Where's that first-class plane ticket at now, Tootie? Funny that you're responsible for finding your way there after you sign your name on the dotted line."

"It's similar to how you treat your girlfriends, Shawn. You wine and dine them on your first couple of dates, and then you give them the cold shoulder after they've fallen for you," I said half-jokingly.

"Well, let's hope the University of Georgia doesn't treat you like an old girlfriend," Dad chimed in.

"I doubt they'd ever treat me like that. By the time I'm finished with this school, they'll have a statue of me outside of the stadium," I said, hoping to cover up the anxiety within.

We made it to Georgia in a little less than 8 hours and checked into a local hotel for the night. The next morning, I officially reported to my first college training camp. After introducing myself to other coaches, athletic trainers, student interns, and other staffers at the check-in table, I was assigned to a room in Russell Hall—a freshman dorm where the entire football team would be staying for the three weeks of training camp. I, however, was told I'd be staying there for the whole school year.

I rushed to the third floor to get a glimpse of my room. Right away I saw a tall, skinny kid with dreadlocks, removing items from a black duffel bag.

"Hey, what's up? I assume you're my roommate," I said as I sized him up. "My name is Mike, but everyone calls me Tootie."

After National Signing Day, I'd read up on each new freshman coming in, so I recognized him immediately. His name was Marcus Baker, a five-star recruit from South Carolina, and one of the top defensive backs in the country. He had one of the best highlight films I'd ever seen, even knowing this, I still acted as if I had never heard of him in my life.

"I guess so! My name is Marcus, nice to meet you," he said with a southern accent. "I hope you don't mind me choosing this side of the room."

"You were here first, so it's all yours," I said. "Do you know what we have going on today?"

"We have physicals, lunch, freshman orientation, and team meetings tonight."

We talked for a little longer about our expectations, and being away from home. It was a relief to know Marcus had some of the same uncertainties. But, still, we had the same motivations—the only difference being he had a two-year-old son back home. He put even more pressure on himself to use this university as a stepping stone to reach the next level so he could provide a better life for his son.

After hauling all my belongings into the dorm and un-packing, it was time for the moment I was dreading—to say goodbye to Dad and Shawn. Internally, I thought it would be similar to when I waved goodbye to Shawn from the courtroom years ago.

I think he could sense how I felt at that moment, because he pulled me in for a hug and said, "It's time to man up, lil bro. The goals you've set for yourself are here, so go and get them."

After Shawn released me, Dad grabbed me by the shoulders and looked me in the eyes.

"I've been preparing you for this day your entire life, continue making your mom proud." There was no way I could let a tear slide down my face, but God knows I wanted to. I didn't feel quite as sad as I'd felt when Shawn was sent to prison, but it was close. I watched them get into the car and drive away before I pounded on my chest twice to let my emotions know they couldn't come out to play today.

7 FIRST IMPRESSION

TO SAY I FELT LIKE a fish out of water would be an understatement. There was so much information to process. Our academic advisors had facilitated the freshman orientation the previous night. They explained eligibility rules, the university's code of conduct, and mandatory study hall requirements. That was all I could remember before I lost focus and began to daydream. Our team meeting was much different. Coach Stuart's demeanor does not allow for anyone to daydream. He demanded our undivided attention—I'd feel sorry for anyone who was caught staring off into space while he was talking. Let's just say he seemed much nicer on my recruiting visit.

He let it be known to the entire team that every starting position was up for grabs, no matter if you were a freshman or a senior. He didn't care about what anyone had done in the past. His goal was to put the best eleven guys on the field in hopes of becoming national champions. After meeting as a team, we broke off and met with our position coaches. Our running back coach, Coach White, was young, energetic, and an excellent communicator from what I could tell. He reiterated the team's expectations before giving us his. Coach wanted us to be receptive to coaching, take care of the small things, and always give all we had—and he promised to do the same.

We had a total of eight running backs fighting for one starting spot. When I introduced myself to the other seven guys, I received a warm welcome. And honestly, it was a much better reception than I thought I would get, considering the disrespectful greeting that was handed to me from Dominque Jones during my recruiting visit. He was also in the meeting room, which prompted me to prepare for the worst. I thought the competition for a starting spot would create an "everybody for self" type of culture. You know, the kind of environment where you secretly pray on the downfall of your teammates so you can become the man to be featured in the limelight. But the guys, including Dominque, all said they were glad I chose the university.

They even went as far as to enlighten me on the running back tradition of eating dinner together every night of training camp.

Not a bad start, I thought.

I woke up at 5:00 a.m. to head to breakfast before our 8:00 a.m. practice. The spread left nothing to be desired. It consisted of buttermilk pancakes, waffles, grits, fresh fruit, and a chef preparing omelets right before your eyes. I only ate two eggs and a banana. I would've devoured more, but my stomach felt a bit queasy from the buildup of nerves.

Those feelings quickly turned into pure excitement after entering the locker room. It was like Christmas in July. Our lockers were filled with the latest Nike gear: four pairs of football cleats, eight pairs of gloves, and enough University of Georgia football apparel to open a shopping mall. But the cherry on top was the sight of my jersey number. There, hung two practice jerseys inside my locker, displaying the famous number seven on them. I

felt like Clark Kent, but after I put on my number seven
jersey to head onto the practice field, I felt more like Su-
perman. *I'm ready now.*

Our first practice in only helmets was slow-paced and
full of instruction. Everything I'd learned in high school
was useless to me. Coach White corrected everything
from my positional stance, to how I took a hand-off from
the quarterback. Things that once felt natural were dis-
sected and altered to the way Coach wanted to see them
done.

"Tootie, you are carrying the ball like a loaf of bread,"
Coach White said before demonstrating how he wanted
the football handled. "It should be high on your breast
plate and tight enough that a defender can't take it away.
If you fumble, your butt will be back in Virginia Beach
catching a tan."

I turned my head and gave him a dumbfounded look.

"You think I'm joking? Let that ball hit the turf and
see what happens."

He made me repeat the running back drill about seven
times. His way of carrying the football felt so odd; I kept
reverting to the way I'd always carried it. In an attempt to

keep Coach from embarrassing me once more, I made a conscious effort to carry the ball "high and tight"—just like he preached.

As an upperclassman with more experience, Dominque was doing everything correctly. I could tell by the praise he was getting from Coach after leading every drill. "That's how you finish, Dominque!" Or there was, "Way to set the tone."

To keep myself out of the doghouse with Coach, I started following everything Dominque was doing. When he didn't take a water break after an exhausting drill, I didn't take one either. When he finished each drill by running an additional ten yards, I ran twelve. And when he showed enthusiasm for teammates who made plays or finished a drill strongly, I matched his energy by doing the same.

After catching on, Dominique leaned over. "I see you thought I wasn't joking when I said you were going to be my understudy on your recruiting visit."

"You have to know how to follow before you can lead," I replied. "I'm trying to get better, so I'm following you as the leader."

My dad always told me to find the hardest working person in the room and outwork them. If Dominque was the front-runner to get the starting nod, so be it. But I wasn't going to allow it to be an easy decision for the coaches. I was going to make this dude earn his starting spot.

Coach White pulled us all together. "We're about to pick up the pace during our next team drill. We're going head-to-head against our linebackers and defensive backs. It's simple, don't allow the defender to stop you from catching the pass. With that said, win every snap, fellas. Break down on me, win on three—one...two...three...."

"Win!" we all screamed, before heading down to the opposite side of the field.

Dominque was up first. He lined up against our all-conference linebacker, Keith Riddick. Think of the scariest bad guy from a horror film and multiply that by ten and you have Keith. The guy was intimidating. Imagine how much more frightening he became once we put on shoulder pads and helmets. I'd seen plenty of big guys in high school, but I'd yet to see any as big as him that could move as quickly as he could. I thought my high school drills were competitive, but there was no comparison. Guys were willing to risks their lives before losing to a teammate in an individual drill.

"These boys don't know what they just got themselves into!" Keith screamed in the direction of our running back group. Tension was as thick as the Georgia heat. Terrell signaled the pass route to Dominque. Dominique nodded back to Terrell to let him know "he got it." Every step Dominque took, Keith matched him stride for stride. Terrell let the ball go after seeing a small opening for Dominque to catch it. As the ball arrived in Dominque's hands, he pulled it into his chest to secure the catch, but not before Keith's large hand swatted it to the ground.

"No sir, not on my watch! Take that weak mess back down the opposite end of the field," Keith said triumphantly. "Was that the best you guys could do?"

I knew exactly what to do to set myself apart early in our running back competition. Instead of lining up against another linebacker, I dropped back in line to ensure I'd be matched up against Keith. Not only did I want to compete against the best, but I wanted to measure myself against the elite players. When Keith saw we'd be matched up, he screamed, "Are you guys trying to waste my time or something? I eat freshmen for dinner."

I huddled up with Terrell and said, "Just throw it out there. I'll go and get it."

Terrell did just that. I took off, leaving Keith in my rearview as Terrell let a rocket go in the air. I chased the ball down and hauled in the pass. On my way back down the field, I stopped in front of Keith and said, "Eat that." Angry and slightly embarrassed for letting a freshman beat him for a touchdown, Keith responded with, "Wait until we put on pads."

DOG DAYS OF SUMMER

IT'D BEEN THIRTEEN DAYS SINCE the start of fall camp, but it felt like six months. I couldn't even tell you what day of the week it was. Every day was Groundhog Day. It felt like we did the same thing every day. We ate breakfast, went to meetings, practiced, ate lunch, napped, lifted weights, practiced again, ate dinner, and then met for one last time.

Each time we met, we watched film of the practice before. Coach White always said, "The film doesn't lie." He didn't miss a thing, either, pointing out the smallest of mistakes in front of the other seven guys in our position room. On days I practiced well, I didn't mind watching film. But even then, Coach pointed out how I could do things better. On the days I practiced terribly, I wanted to wear earplugs. During one particular meeting, I'd heard *piss poor effort, timid, soft, lazy, and bad* directed toward me. I don't remember Coach's exact words, but it went something this, "Tootie, this was nothing but a piss poor effort. Look at yourself. You look timid, soft, and lazy. You may have been the man at your high school, but looking at this play, I don't see how. This is as bad as it gets."

Ouch. Funny how you always hear nobody is perfect throughout life, but in football the standard is perfection.

Our meetings were a humbling experience; I quickly learned not to get too high or too down on myself. On top of feeling a constant déjà vu, I was homesick. Dad had known exactly what he was doing when he told me I wasn't allowed to bring my car. I missed my family and Sophia so much. I hadn't spoken to anyone on the phone longer than thirty minutes. All of my free time was spent napping, studying our playbook, or spending time with athletic trainers, trying to quickly recover my body from one practice to the next.

My position on the depth chart changed by the day. I'd been listed as high as two, and as low as number eight. Although I hated to admit it, Dominque had had the better camp so far. Early on, I thought I was leading the pack.

But like Coach had said, the film didn't lie. I struggled with learning blitz protections and holding onto the football. I'd made more plays than Dominque, but I'd also made more mistakes. Coach had said he couldn't trust me in a game because he didn't know what Tootie he'd get. There was the good Tootie, where I'd break for 50-yard runs against our defense, then there was the bad Tootie, where I'd forget what play was called or let our middle linebacker sack our All-American quarterback.

My toughest day by far was the first day in full pads. I thought Keith had forgotten the embarrassment he'd felt when I beat him deep for a touchdown. Every drill we ran that day, he wanted to be matched up against me. He wanted to instill fear. I didn't back down; I wanted him to respect me. We went at it as soon as practice started. All day I competed against this monster. For the most part, I'd held my own. But during the team scrimmage, he regained bragging rights.

Our offense was at the goal line, one yard out from the end zone. One play prior, I'd taken a screen pass for thirty yards. I almost scored before being tackled at the one-yard line. My confidence was up. Making a huge play after already winning battles throughout practice against Keith was setting me apart from the rest of the running backs. The next play called was a handoff right up the middle. After I took the handoff, my eyes lit up like a Christmas tree after I saw a small gap to the end zone. As I made my move, there was Keith. He hit me so hard that my mind went blank for a quick second. I fumbled the football. When the stars stopped spinning around my head, I looked up, and our defense was running toward the opposite end with it. Coach didn't send me back to Virginia Beach, but he did send me to the bottom of the depth chart.

Today was a major relief. Coach Stuart informed the team at breakfast that he was giving us the morning off. There were no meetings, practices, or weightlifting. I couldn't remember the last time I was this excited. The only thing I wanted to do was sleep. But before I could do that, I had to meet with my academic advisor to register for classes. Hopefully, it wouldn't take any more than thirty minutes.

"Hello, Mr. Hernandez," I said nervously as I walked into his office. "I'm Michael Mayberry, and I'm here to register for classes."

"I know exactly who you are, Tootie. Have a seat and let's get to know each other a bit."

There goes my nap, I thought.

"Yes, sir," I said as I took a seat.

"So, Tootie, I have a couple of objectives for you. First, I want you to stay eligible, and to do that you must maintain a 2.0 GPA. Secondly, I want you to graduate. A degree will open so many doors. Lastly, I want you to choose a major that is rewarding."

There was that word again. No way would I be able to escape it.

"I don't know much about majors. I mean, I never gave much thought to it before."

"And that's okay, Tootie. You don't have to choose a major until your sophomore year."

"Whew," I said, feeling relieved.

"But I do want you to start thinking about it. As you go through your first year, write down what appeals to you. Think about the things you enjoy learning about. We can meet periodically and discuss your thoughts and formulate your career path."

"My career path?"

"Yes! Remember when I said my objective is for you to choose a rewarding major?"

"Yes, sir," I replied.

"What I'm referring to is this: for example, if in four or five years you come back and say, 'I'm glad I chose to major in accounting, because now I'm opening up my own accounting firm called Tootie CPA'—this would be rewarding because your degree led you to a career. A college degree is not what it was yesterday. You have to have a plan. I see so many athletes taking the easy road out and majoring in something that doesn't transfer well into the real world. Take advantage of this opportunity, Tootie."

"In four to five years, I plan on being in the—"

"NFL," he finished.

"Exactly."

"I don't doubt it for one second, Tootie. I've seen a couple of practices this summer, and you have the tools to make it. Let's say you get drafted after your junior year and play for ten years. You will be around thirty-two when you retire. What will you do for the rest of your life?"

"I don't know," I said.

"This is just something for you to think about. If you can see yourself in the NFL three years from now, continue using your vision—envision what you will be doing twenty years from now."

"I don't think anyone's ever put it that way before."

"So what I'm going to do is register you for all of your core classes. But remember what I said: start thinking about what appeals to you."

As I was walking back to my dorm room and replaying the conversation, I started to think that maybe I should apply myself to academics more than I did in high school. *Maybe I should major in something like finance or engineering.* Those thoughts only lasted five minutes. I entered my dorm room, plopped down on my mattress, closed my eyes, and drifted away into an exhausted sleep.

9 SCHOOL'S IN SESSION

I PEELED A BANANA AND devoured it to get something in my stomach as I walked 15 minutes across campus with Marcus to our football facility. If not for the chirping birds, the campus would be as quiet as a mouse. Other students were still passed out. They didn't have to wake for a few more hours to make their 8:00 a.m. classes—if they even had one.

I threw on my black shorts and shirt, then headed directly into the weight room before our 5:30 a.m. start time. As we settled into our workout, the walls echoed with teammates grunting, weights clanking, and strength coaches hollering during each lift to push us beyond our capabilities.

"Last rep, Tootie. Push, push, push, great job!"

Three hundred pounds later....

It takes a lot to get going this early, but I had no choice. There were three time slots to choose from: 5:30 a.m., 10:00 a.m., and 1:00 p.m. The upperclassmen got first choice, mostly selecting the later time slots, leaving the freshmen stuck with waking up as early as 4:30 a.m. to make mandatory lift sessions on time.

"Man, y'all not going to shower?" I yelled in our locker room.

"My first class is on the other side of campus, and I haven't eaten breakfast yet," one of my teammates responded. "It's either be funky, or take a shower and be late. Just my luck one of the coaches will be doing class checks. I'll choose funky. I don't want extra sprints at practice because I'm tardy."

Luckily for me, my 8:00 a.m. science class wasn't too far from our locker room. I showered in a hurry and headed over to one of the dining halls to swipe my student ID for breakfast. Growing up with a single dad, I often ate Pop-Tarts, so having access to so many dining options was by far my favorite part of college.

"What in the world is this?" I said to myself, surveying the scene—over 100 students packed into a science class that was the size of my high school auditorium.

I took a seat next to a young lady wearing a University of Georgia baseball cap.

"Hi, I'm Jennifer. Do you play football here?" she asked.

I automatically assumed she was asking because I was a black male in college, but then I realized my University of Georgia football t-shirt was giving it away.

"Hi Jennifer, I'm Tootie. And yes, I play football here."

"I'll be at the first game this Saturday. What's your number so I can cheer you on?"

Her question embarrassed me. All it did was remind me that I didn't beat Dominque out for the starting spot. I felt like I let myself down by not accomplishing my goal, and the thought of not being anyone to cheer for boiled my blood.

"I'm number seven," I said. "Not sure if I will give you much to cheer about. I don't expect to play much."

"Your time will come, plus I can say I've been rooting you on the whole time—before you become too popular," she said. "Aren't we playing a nationally ranked team or something like that?"

"Yes, we're playing Clemson, who is ranked fourth in the country," I replied.

Our conversation was interrupted by the introduction of our instructor. He talked just as I expected: monotone and long-winded. While the instructor lectured, Jennifer took notes on almost everything he was saying. I couldn't believe how fast she processed the information. I subconsciously felt judged by her for just sitting there, so I started to take notes, too, but was lost in determining the critical facts from the unimportant ones. I'd about lost all hope in this school thing already, until Jennifer said she would provide me a copy of her notes.

After science class ended, I had a couple of options of how I could spend my hour off before my next class. I could go back to my dorm room and take a cat nap. I wasn't entirely exhausted, but the thought of what I had to do for the rest of the day made the nap seem much more appealing. Skipping the nap and going back to the football facility to watch film on Clemson was another option. But the expectation of not playing much made that seem like a waste of time. There was a slim chance Dominque could get injured, or play horribly, which would open up the opportunity for me to play. With that idea in mind, it was important for me to be ready.

"Number 56 for Clemson is some trash. I hope we run at him all game," I heard Terrell say to Dominque as I entered the film room.

"What's up, Tootie? How was the first day of class?" Dominque asked.

"Not bad. Did you have a class yet?"

"Nope, watching film is my class this week," Dominque responded. "I've been waiting for this opportunity my entire life. This is my first chance to start, and I have to seize the moment. We're going to play on national television against a top five ball club that is probably going to have a professional scout from every team in attendance, so class is the last thing on my mind right now."

I was quickly starting to recognize the magnitude of the game build as we approached Saturday's kickoff. It was only Monday, but the atmosphere around campus was buzzing. There were posters of Terrell everywhere I turned. Several students were wearing his jersey, and, to top it off, I'd seen several flyers promoting certain destinations to be the official "after game party." It had only been a couple of hours into my first day of college, and already I was struggling to compartmentalize between preparing for a game, and getting the hang of this school thing.

I left the film room in time to catch the bus across campus for my 10:00 a.m. math class. While walking into class, I realized I was in the wrong building on the wrong side of campus. *I must've misread my map.* The next bus wasn't coming for at least twenty minutes, and class was set to start in five minutes. I broke out into a full sprint.

Out of all the people I could've run into, it happened to be Coach White. He was on a casual jog—and was running toward my direction. I tried avoiding him by walking across the street, but that only made it more obvious.

"Come here, Tootie," he demanded. "Why aren't you in class?"

I explained how I misread the map, thinking he would understand, being that it was the first day of class and all.

"You've been here all summer, and you could've easily asked someone to make sure you were in the right place. I will see you after practice."

So much for that thought....

As much as I wanted to plead my case, I refrained. I learned from my dad not to sound argumentative with those in authority, so I took my loss and kept tracking to class. I arrived about fifteen minutes late, but unlike high school, college instructors appeared to be unbothered by it. I took a seat in the back of the room as the math instructor posed a question to the class.

"The sum of two numbers is 2, the product of the same two numbers is 3. What is the sum of the reciprocals of the two numbers?"

"Aww, here we go," I mumbled.

But he broke down the concept on his whiteboard in a way that I quickly understood. Nice change of pace to have a teacher who didn't lure me to sleep. I felt accomplished in the fact that I learned something.

I called Sophia following class. "Good morning, how's your day going so far?"

"It's going pretty good, but I can't talk right now, my class is about to start. Can I call you later?" she asked.

"Yes, but I have a psychology class after lunch and then practice, so if I don't pick up, I'll call you tonight."

Isn't there an old saying about making time for what you want? Between leaving for Georgia and Sophia starting class at James Madison University, there hadn't been enough time in the day. We talked for a couple minutes here and there, but it was all surface details. It used to be that if we weren't together, we were on the phone. It was certainly a different vibe with us being hundreds of miles away from each other.

My growling stomach wouldn't let me mope over Sophia any longer. I headed over to the closest dining hall for lunch. I had a little over an hour to eat and start on math homework before my last class of the day at 1:00 p.m. I threw down some barbeque chicken, mashed potatoes, and green beans before I started to feel drained. Any thought of starting homework went flying out the window. I could barely keep myself from yawning. I was either exhausted due to a full stomach, or because I knew I had to sit in another hour-long class.

My head in psychology class rocked back and forth.

"The gentleman in the back nodding off, please come up here to the front," the instructor called out.

I looked around the room, then back to the professor. "Who, me?"

"Yes, you," he responded.

I got up and walked at a snail's pace, hoping he would say never mind because of the time I wasted. Awkward and embarrassing doesn't even begin to cover how I felt. The instructor didn't stop me as I reached the front.

We introduced ourselves, and Instructor Gray looked to the class. "Besides our ethnicity, what is another difference between Michael and me?" The looks on my classmates' faces were of confusion, and I bet I had the same look on mine. Everyone hesitated.

Instructor Gray broke the silence. "This is a cultural diversity psychology class and some topics will cause tension, and that's okay if we all respect one another and keep an open mind."

I still didn't know where he was going with this one. He took a step closer and placed his hand on my shoulder. "Besides our race, there isn't a difference. Once we understand our differences, we will understand how much we are alike. During this semester, we will take a deep dive into cultural diversity."

He dismissed the class shortly thereafter, so I started to walk off.

"Michael, you can learn a great deal in my class if you are awake."

"Yes, sir," I responded with a tone to unwelcome further conversation. Instructor Gray definitely knew my name, so my best bet was to stay awake in the future.

I checked my phone: 1:45 p.m. With over an hour before the start of team meetings, I headed toward the player lounge inside of our locker room.

"I got next," I hollered to a couple of teammates who were playing pool. After two games of knocking the 8-ball into the corner pocket, I prepared for team meetings and practice by jumping into the hot tub, then getting my ankles taped.

"I don't have to tell you all how big this game is," Coach Stuart said as he opened up our team meeting. "You can feel it across campus. Stay focused, practice hard, and take care of your business throughout the week, and on game day, everything will play out in our favor."

The intensity of practice was there, but it was very different compared to summer practices. Summer practices were physical and designed to break us down mentally. Practices during a game week were fast-paced with less tackling. Since I was the second-string running back, I rarely got reps with our first-team offense. All first-team reps went to Dominque, with me sparing him when a breather was needed. I occasionally slapped Dominque on the helmet and said "good job" in between team breaks. I assumed this was what backups did…? Although my pride was hurt for not starting, I still wanted to see us win.

After an excellent practice, we met at midfield to break down as a team. While Coach Stuart gave his final thoughts on our performance, my mind was focused on showering, eating, and getting to bed. Noticeably missing from that list was homework and study hall. I probably had at least two hours' worth of reading to do, but it was 6:00 p.m. and my exhaustion had reached a new level. If I could get to bed by 9:00 p.m., that'd be considered a success. As far as homework went, I'd hopefully find some time to complete it the following morning.

After our break down, we rushed to the locker room, but not before the sound of a whistle pierced my ears.

"Tootie, I hope you don't think I forgot," Coach White yelled. "Come on back. You owe me extra sprints for being late on the first day of class. Shame on you!"

10 NOT IN OUR HOUSE

"TOOTIE!" MARCUS SCREAMED. "Wake up, bro, you are shivering and breathing heavily."

I shot up to find my bed drenched in sweat. It was 3:00 a.m., and I was already feeling anxious. I was always a nervous wreck before big games, but the nerves were hitting me early.

"Are you good?" Marcus asked.

"Yeah, man, thanks for waking me."

"I thought you were hyperventilating or something."

"I was having a nightmare."

"About what?"

"Our game was tied in the fourth quarter. The ball was going to me on the next play, but I couldn't remember what I was supposed to do. That's all I remember before you woke me up."

"Well if it makes you feel any better, I haven't slept one bit, either. Man, we are playing our first college game on national television tomorrow," Marcus said.

"It's crazy to think we're here already."

"Yeah, it is. I've been reminding myself that I've been doing this all my life, and that tomorrow is just another game."

Sure, it was another game, but I'd never played in front of a hundred thousand people before. Marcus had nothing to worry about. He was one of the best players on the team. The guy was nothing short of spectacular. I thought I was the best athlete on the planet until I saw him. He'd been shutting down each receiver on our team, and I expected nothing less tomorrow.

I eventually fell back to sleep, only realizing it after I awoke a couple hours later. I felt refreshed and mentally sharp. I knew my nightmare was just that, and if I got called on tonight, I'd be ready.

The game day agenda was compact. We had breakfast, meetings, lunch, more meetings, dinner, "Dawg Walk," and a lot of waiting before kickoff. To kill time between team functions, I decided to call family. First up: Dad.

"Please make sure you record the game tonight," I told him.

"I sure will! Sorry I couldn't make it to your first college game, but there will be plenty of others I'll be at."

"It's okay, not sure how much I will touch the field tonight anyways," I said, sounding repetitive.

"Do I have to tell the piano story about your mother again?" my dad said. "Stay ready."

After our team breakfast and meetings, I called Shawn. But before I could say hello—

"Man, y'all are a 7-point underdog tonight."

"I don't pay that stuff any mind, big bro. Predictions don't win games. Are you going to watch tonight?"

"Am I going to watch? That's not even a question. I'll have my number seven Georgia jersey on."

By lunchtime, the enthusiasm on campus had heightened. Parking lots were filled with tents and tailgating fans. Sweet aromas filled the air—everything from burgers to slaughtered pigs. The upperclassmen appeared to be unfazed by all the festivities as we walked into our "team only" lunch. My eyes were filled with amazement. I was focused on tonight's game, but also soaking in this experience.

During our last meeting before the game, we met with our position coaches for a quick assignment check.

"Tootie, what do you do on strong right z-motion 865 Cadillac?" Coach White asked.

Without hesitation, I said, "I check for the blitzing linebacker, if he doesn't blitz, then I swing to the right."

"Good job," Coach White praised.

My nightmare initially had me bugging, but after our assignment check, I was confident that I knew what I was supposed to do. Coach wanted us to stay off our feet and relax until team dinner, so I went back to bed and dialed up Sophia.

We talked over an hour and caught up on all that had been eluding us these past several months. Sophia had made a seamless transition to college life, which didn't come as a surprise. It was good to hear how happy she was with the university. She expressed how much she missed me, and I did the same. She filled me in on her plans to visit so she could see me "kill it" on the big stage, as she had always done before. Sophia had a calming personality that made stress, pressure, or problems seem small. Not once during our hour-long conversation did I think about what was at hand tonight.

At our pre-game dinner, Coach Stuart gathered everyone's attention and introduced the team to a young pastor named Randy Beckett. After being introduced, Randy stood directly in the middle of the dining area and told us about his background. Judging by the looks on my teammates' faces, everyone was disinterested—including myself.

Our expressions quickly changed when Randy screamed, "Look around, who has your back?"

We all surveyed the room and turned our attention back to him.

"In a couple more hours, remember that you are not at this alone. Your teammates have your back, but more importantly, God has your back, too. Isaiah 41:10 says, "So do not fear, for I am with you; do not be dismayed, for I am your God. I will strengthen you and help you; I will uphold you with my righteous right hand."

I rarely went to church as a kid besides the occasional Easter Sundays, but I always believed in God. Randy's message was clear: *God is with me, and I don't have to fear. I can play my game without any cares.*

We were getting closer and closer to kickoff, two-and-a-half hours to be exact. We boarded our team buses in preparation for the "Dawg Walk." The walk would allow fans to get a final glimpse of the team before we walked into the stadium to prepare for battle.

Dominque leaned in. "Brace yourself, Tootie."

I imagined the walk to be a stroll while waving at our fans as they screamed "good luck." But, Dominque was right in telling me to brace myself. Once we stepped off the bus, the atmosphere was electric. Thousands of fans packed each side of the street, screaming as loud as the marching band was playing. While nobody called out my name as they did Terrell's, I did hear this several times: "Good luck out there tonight, #7."

The locker room was the total opposite of the Dawg Walk. You could hear a pin drop. My teammates mentally prepared by listening to music through their headphones, or by sitting in silence, most likely going through game scenarios in their head.

As for me, I'd been back and forth between sitting silently at my locker and sitting on the toilet. The wait until kickoff had gotten the best of my stomach. A couple minutes before kickoff, Coach Stuart huddled the team in the middle of the locker room.

"Ten years from now, you will still be thinking about this game tonight. When you look back, how do you want it to be remembered? You have the opportunity to create a legend tonight. You do that by leaving nothing and taking everything. Give it all you got while taking everything away from them. If you do that, I promise the legacy of this football team will remain forever."

Coach Stuart's words resonated in all of us. We ran out of the tunnel onto the field, inspired as the stadium erupted. I'd scored game-winning touchdowns, had been named the most valuable player on many teams, but none of those moments could match the feeling of running onto the field.

Midway through the second quarter, we found ourselves in a tightly contested ballgame. The game was all tied up at seven. Other than a touchdown pass from Terrell, our offense had not been able to move the ball with any consistency. Even though Dominque had played every snap of the game, his impact has been insignificant. I had yet to touch the field, but I felt that could change at any minute. I caught a glimpse of Coach Stuart and Coach White huddling on our sideline. I moved closer with the hopes of overhearing their conversation. Even over the raucous crowd, I could've sworn I heard Coach Stuart say, "Get Tootie in the game."

Unfortunately, the message was not relayed to me, because on the very next play, Dominque busted up the sideline for a thirty-yard touchdown run, giving us a 14–7 lead over Clemson. Internally, there was a heavy dose of envy. I was a second away from taking Dominque's place in the game before his touchdown. Once again, he did just enough to keep me on the sideline.

Externally, I was happy for him. I was the first person to congratulate him as he trotted back to our sideline. We jumped and chest bumped, and after we landed, I smacked the back of his helmet. "Great run, keep it up."

At halftime, the locker room was filled with confidence.

"One more half, one more half," Terrell encouraged.

Neither Coach Stuart nor Coach White approached me about playing. I assumed I'd misheard them earlier on the sideline, or it was called off after Dominque elevated his game. Either way, I decided to put my selfishness aside and become Dominque's biggest cheerleader during the next half.

We got off to an excellent start. Terrell was firing on all cylinders, marching us down Clemson's throat. We were twenty yards out from scoring another touchdown that would put us up to a commanding 21–7 lead. Smelling blood, Terrell hurried the offense to the line of scrimmage and dropped back to pass the football. Not seeing anyone open and alluding a tackler, Terrell threw a dart across the field to Dominque in the end zone. Dominque jumped to catch the pass, but before he landed, one of Clemson's defensive players hit his legs, causing him to flip and land on his shoulder and neck. The referees threw up both of their arms signaling a touchdown, but Dominque remained on the ground, motionless. It was as if time had stopped.

Our team crowded around in silence as tears flowed from seeing how severely injured he was. After about twenty minutes, the ambulance picked him up. The good news was that he eventually moved his legs and arms. Even though we were up by 14 points, the air in the building left in the ambulance with Dominque. Clemson marched right down the field to bring the game within a touchdown.

"Tootie, not much needs to be said at this point. You've been doing this your whole life, so let the world see it," Coach White said calmly.

Last year at this time, I was playing for Bayside High School, and now all of a sudden, millions of people were about to watch my first college play. To stop the intrusive thoughts of wondering what my dad, brother, Sophia, and others are thinking as they watched me on television, I began to tell myself over and over that I was built for this.

As we huddled, Terrell looked directly into my eyes. "Welcome to prime time, Tootie."

"Terrell, I was built for this."

"OK, here we go, fellas. Spread zaps right, Z to X trade, 36 zone red," Terrell said.

After hearing the ball would be coming to me, the crowd became deaf to my ears. I couldn't hear anything but my rapidly beating heartbeat. I stood behind Terrell in formation and gauged the field in what felt like slow motion. While surveying, I noticed where I thought an opening might be once the play started. Terrell handed me the ball, and as I moved in that direction, everything went from slow to fast in the blink of an eye. The opening I'd anticipated closed, and I ran directly to our sideline for a loss of a yard. Coach Stuart ran up to me as fast as he could and grabbed my facemask.

"What in the heck was that? Are you scared? Get your head in the game, son." Actually, there were some profanities mixed in.

Profanities or not, his words refocused me. I was able to take a deep breath and slow the game down mentally. To my surprise, the coaches called another run intended for me on the very next play. This time I didn't anticipate, but instead reacted to what the defense gave me. I gained ten yards on the play and started to feel a boost of confidence. Unfortunately, the drive to the end zone was interrupted by an interception thrown by Terrell on the next play. That was just the beginning of our downfall. Clemson eventually staged a comeback, beating us 35–21.

After the clock struck zero, I walked off the field with a heavy heart, but my head held high. There was no further word on Dominque's status. Regardless, I knew it would be at least several weeks before he could play again. I'd most likely become the starting running back until then.

11

NO REST FOR THE WEARY

WHILE MOST OF MY TEAMMATES partied to cope with the loss, I was in no mood. I turned off my phone immediately after the game—I hated being directly attached to a loss. If I hadn't touched the field, the loss would've been easier to stomach. I decided to sit in my dorm room and think about the what ifs. *What if I would've scored last night? Would that have affected the outcome? What if Dominque had never gotten hurt? Would we have won?* The thought of us not scoring again after his injury was on my mind until I drifted off to sleep.

I woke up to over 250 text messages. Most were from people back home. I received everything from *you looked terrific on television last night* to *dang, did your teammate break his neck?* I intended to respond to each one of them until I remembered that I had a science exam to study for.

After about an hour of reading through my textbook and notes, the material became meaningless words. My thoughts kept going back and forth between why I didn't make a better move against the defender on 3rd and three, to trying to remember the definitions of anabolism and catabolism. On top of that, my body felt like it was involved in a car wreck. On the bright side, we had two days to mentally and physically recover. Tonight we'd have team meetings, which would likely include a bunch of verbal butt chewing's from our coaching staff. Aside from weightlifting, we'd have Monday off. We'd officially start preparation on Tuesday morning for our Saturday game against Tennessee.

Before our meeting, the majority of my teammates sat in the athletic training room, icing aches and pains and asking team trainers to look over injuries more thoroughly. With ice bags on both shoulders, Terrell leaned over and said, "I played horribly last night."

"We all could have played better, Terrell," I reassured.

"I don't think you get it, Tootie. I watched highlights on ESPN this morning, and they didn't say Georgia played bad. They highlighted and analyzed my worst throws while saying I played awful—not the team, me."

Man, and I thought I put a lot of pressure on myself. Terrell had me beat. Sensing he needed some encouragement, I said, "The world always seems like it's about to be over after a loss, but as soon as you throw for 300 yards against Tennessee next week, all will be forgotten."

Every member of our team had a dejected look on their face as we filled in the seats of the meeting room. We all knew what was about to happen as we waited for Coach to enter and kickoff the meeting. My expectation was there would be kicking over trashcans or the type of yelling from Coach Stuart that would make the person on the front row wish they had an umbrella to protect them from the spit projecting from his mouth.

When Coach Stuart entered, you could hear the deep exhales as we prepared for the tirade. However, he entered the room pushing a cart filled with cupcakes. He stopped in front of each person and asked them if they wanted vanilla or chocolate. By the time he got to me, I had yet to see one person eat their cupcake or make a sound. I asked for chocolate and spent the rest of the time staring at mine as he finished passing them around.

"There's no need to make a scene about the embarrassing performance we put on last night. Let's just enjoy our cupcakes," Coach Stuart said. After we scarfed them down, he went on to say, "Sometimes in life, you are what you eat—or in our case, we eat what we play like." Coach dismissed the team to watch the film with our positional coaches and didn't say another word. I wasn't sure if it was some reverse psychology, or a motivational tactic, but it left our team even angrier about how we'd played. Had there been a game tonight, I bet we would've played like our lives depended on it.

"What are you doing on this play, Tootie? Watch yourself; you look like a chicken with its head cut off." Or it was, "This is not what I coached you to do."

After the game, I was pissed that we'd lost, but I felt like I'd played well. Even friends from back home texted me and said I did. But, the way Coach White dogged each play of mine made me feel unworthy to wear the red-colored jersey. It bothered me to the point that I stayed behind after everyone left to chat with him.

"It always seems like I don't do anything right. Even when I gain twenty yards, you say I should've done this or that instead," I expressed.

"Tootie, my job is to make you better. There is always more you could've done. You have so much potential, and if I don't try and pull it out, then I'm wasting both of our time."

"I understand," I said, then turned to leave.

I was one step from exiting the meeting room before Coach stopped me. "Dominque is not going to play football again, so the keys are yours going forward. What will you do with them?"

I replayed his words before turning around in shock. "Hold up, he's not playing?"

"No, he isn't," Coach White answered. "You know that old saying about if a coach doesn't say anything at all, then you should be worried? Get used to me riding you."

I left feeling bittersweet. My goal was to come here and start as a freshman, but I didn't want to earn the job that way. Even more so, I was taken aback by what Coach had said about Dominque. *Did he mean he was done for the season, or done forever?* I was heartbroken by the fact that Dominque was looking like a first-round draft pick one minute, and the next he was on the ground lifeless with his football career in jeopardy.

I called my dad to relay the news, but before I could get a word in—

"I was trying to reach you all night last night. Anyway, I'm glad you called because I want to tell you that you looked like the moment was too big for you last night."

Typical words from my straight-shooting father. I didn't expect a "good game" from him, but a "hello" would've been nice. Normally out of respect I let my dad state his piece, but today I was not feeling it.

"Please, not right now, Dad. I'm tired, and I've had an earful already."

We sat in silence for at least a minute, and every second that went by, I became more and more infuriated. "As a matter of fact, Dad, what you didn't see on television was the different emotions I had to deal with during the game. One minute I thought I was going to provide a spark, then the next minute Dominque scores. Should I celebrate or be disappointed? Then, after that, I thought I wasn't going to touch the field, and I wound up seeing my teammate suffer from a career-ending injury. On top of that, we still had a game to play, so, yes, the moment did get bigger than what I thought it would."

That was the first time I'd ever raised my voice to him. It was always "yes, sir" or "no, sir." There was no second-guessing or disrespecting him. You would have thought my dad was a sergeant in the military or something. But, even if my dad didn't mention it in our phone conversation, deep down, I think he admired the way I shut him down.

By the time I got back to my dorm, it was approaching 8:30 p.m. Not overly confident about my science exam, I took another stab at studying. After an hour or so, the thought of having to wake by 5:00 a.m. to make weight-lifting on time made me drowsy.

My dad would always say, *"Approach school like you do football and you will be all right."* More times than not, his message would go in one ear and out the other. I think he knew I had selective hearing because he would follow-up by saying, *"Just as you want to be the best player on the field, you should take the same approach in the classroom."* But, that was easier said than done. For one, obtaining good grades and being an all-state athlete didn't compare. I was more popular than our high school valedictorian. Secondly, athletics came naturally. Studying for something that I probably wouldn't remember after taking an exam was the most tedious thing ever.

I thought long and hard about what my academic advisor had to say about the importance of life after football. My mindset was that I'd cross that bridge when I got there. I looked at life game by game, so I couldn't see anything past this Saturday's battle at Tennessee. My only current focus was to pass my science exam with at least a C+ so I wouldn't get off to a lousy start by falling below the eligibility threshold.

As I took my usual seat beside Jennifer the next morning, she looked over and her eyes lit up. "Oh my God, you are amazing. When I saw you in the game, I completely freaked out."

Some of our classmates took notice, so I felt the need to play it cool. "Thank you, Jennifer. Are you ready for this exam?" Deep inside, I relished being praised and admired.

"I better be, I studied all week," she replied.

After starting the exam, I was able to do a process of elimination on the four answers to the first few questions. After eliminating two, it was a 50/50 shot. I didn't feel like I was acing the test, but I was sure I wasn't bombing it, either. I looked over at Jennifer to see how she was faring—she wasn't breaking a sweat. She left her test uncovered and slid closer in my direction. I wasn't sure if it was accidental or not, but there appeared to be an open invitation to cheat.

In high school, I would've rather failed a test on my own merit than ace it by copying someone else's work. Cheating and receiving an A was the equivalent to using steroids and becoming the player of the year. How could anyone find satisfaction in that? However, I was tempted to take a peek at Jennifer's answers to see how mine measured up. She studied for an entire week, while I studied for two hours over the course of two days. As hard as it

was, I refrained and finished my test. I knew I had to manage my time better going forward. Whatever grade I got,
I'd learn to live with it.

12

IN MY ZONE

HAVE YOU EVER BEEN IN a zone, the type of zone where everything you do or touch results in perfection? Being in a zone is Jordan dropping 63 points in a hostile environment like the Boston Garden Arena. It's taking a multiple choice exam and knowing the answer before you see the options below. When you're in the zone, there's nothing that can distract you from performing at the highest levels.

I was in that zone. We were leading Tennessee 42–0 at halftime, and I couldn't believe what I had done already. I thought I was dreaming as I sat near my locker, pinching myself to wake up.

Terrell pulled up a stool next to me, rubbed my head, and said, "I don't think you know what you did out there." I looked at him intently as he continued. "I overheard the coaches talking, and they said you are the only Georgia freshman running back to ever score four touchdowns in a game, let alone in one half."

I could feel my head starting to swell, so I snapped out of it. "I haven't done anything yet." We still had another half to go, and I'd be a fool to rest on my first half accomplishments. That's how you lose focus and risk injury. When Kobe looked at the stat sheet in the game, he scored 81 points and saw he had 26 at the half. I bet he didn't pat himself on the back. I imagine he sat in the locker room at halftime and thought about how he could dominate even more once he got back out on the floor.

As we headed back onto the field, I was still repeating, "I haven't done anything yet." I didn't want a hint of pride to sneak in. I had four touchdowns, but my mindset was to score four more. While jogging to the sideline, Coach White grabbed my shoulder pads and said, "You're done."

His words didn't fully register. "Huh?"

"You're done for the game. There's no chance of them coming back. And if we keep you out there, we risk the chance of someone taking a cheap shot in a game we already have in the bag. Good job out there tonight," Coach White elaborated.

I took off my helmet and gloves, placed them on the bench, and cried tears of joy. There was no indication from the past week of practice that I'd have a game for the ages. That's what makes being in the zone unexplainable. It's unpredictable, but when you come to an end, more often than not, the conclusions are legendary. Here I was, less than four months removed from running on the sideline of Bayside High School in Virginia Beach, to etching my name in the history books at the University of Georgia. For me, this was just the start. I wanted to feel this way after each game.

On top of making history, my dad and Shawn made their way to Athens to see my first college start. The smiles on their faces as I located them in the stands were priceless. I threw up a peace sign and grinned from ear to ear.

The butt kicking we were giving Tennessee didn't slow down until the 4th quarter. The score read 56–14 with less than five minutes on the clock. Our stadium was rocking as fans danced and sang along to every song played through the loudspeakers. It was a sight to behold as we avenged our first defeat.

As a team, we were just as loose and turnt up as the fans. After-party plans were already in the works as Terrell came over to me and said, "You have to come and celebrate with your boy tonight. And I'm not taking no for an answer."

Little did he know, I was already thinking about finally hitting a party and bringing Shawn along. After not graduating high school and spending the last six years in prison, I was sure Shawn would love to experience the college nightlife.

"Yeah, man, I'll come out tonight."

After the game ended, one of the media relations staff members approached me. "Reporters have requested your presence at the post-game press conference to interview you. Can you make it to the media room in fifteen minutes?"

"Absolutely," I responded, then headed into the locker room to finish celebrating with my teammates.

Maybe I was just some naïve freshman, but I didn't know much about press conferences. Apparently, if you performed well in a game, the media would request an interview afterward. To put it in perspective, after a good game at Bayside, I would only talk to our local newspaper writer for a couple of minutes. But as I walked into the media room, the feeling that came over me was very different. Media members from *USA Today*, *New York Times*, *ESPN*, and others wanted to talk to little ol' Tootie from Virginia Beach. Coach Stuart, a couple of other teammates who played well, and I sat at a table on top of a stage-like platform while looking down at flashing bright lights from cameras and phones.

Coach Stuart answered the first couple of questions, then the attention shifted to me. A man in a navy blazer with a brown mustache pointed his pen toward me. "Michael Mayberry, did you know the cameras were pointed at you while you had a moment of tears on the sideline? Can you explain the tears after becoming the first freshman running back in this prestigious university's history to score four touchdowns in a half?"

I had no idea the cameras were on me. Everyone who tuned in had probably seen me crying. If that was the case, I'm glad the reporter asked me so I could let everyone know why I was emotional. I took a deep breath and responded. "I'm not supposed to be here. My mom died when I was very young from cancer. I was raised by a single dad in an area where many kids are swallowed up by the streets before their 16th birthday. To be transparent, my brother was one of those kids. Like I said, I'm not supposed to be here. I beat the odds, and to be here today—and starting as a freshman and accomplishing a feat that not even Herschel Walker did, or any other running back that played here—is the best thing that's ever happened to me."

You could hear a pin drop after I answered the question. I don't know if it was my raw emotion or what, but the reporters gathered themselves and gave a quick standing ovation. Several more questions followed, but I could tell my first impression left a mark. As we were wrapping up the press conference, Coach Stuart said he hadn't seen a room full of media members that quiet in his ten-year tenure at the school.

Later on during the night, as Shawn and I were preparing to meet up with my other teammates before going to a party, they showed a clip of the press conference on TV. I was on the bench crying, followed by my answer to the reporter's question. I looked at Dad and Shawn with my jaw on the floor. Not even a second later, all three of our cell phones started to ring.

"I can't stop you from going out or anything, but after tonight, the narrative about you has changed," my dad said. "You are about to be recognizable, so be careful." I didn't pay much attention to what he was saying. He hadn't seen the week I'd had. First, there was the hours of film I watched on my own time, to the long, mentally gruesome practices. Not to mention studying for math and psychology exams while anxiously waiting to hear that I'd received a B on my science exam. *It's only right I celebrate a week of accomplishments. And, I'm always going to be the same me.* Touchdown or riding the pine, I wouldn't change if two people or five million knew my name.

I took a couple steps into the party and was met with slews of cheers, high fives, fist pumps, and beers on the house. It didn't take much for the student body to recognize me. *I wonder what it will be like after a couple more* Sports Center *cameos.* I tried not to let all the attention affect me, but I'd been dreaming about this moment since I was a kid. This was my chance to be the big man on campus.

What made the moment even more special was having Shawn as my wingman. We missed out on these experiences growing up. I was supposed to be the little brother in high school who spent time with the big brother on a college campus. He was supposed to sneak me into his college parties and show me the way college was done. The script had been flipped. Instead, tonight I'd get to show him what college parties were like. I'd get to show him how college kids relieved stress on the weekends, and I felt the need to make this night epic for Shawn.

He fit right in. Six years in prison did not affect his appearance. He was still the handsome, charming guy I always knew. As the night went on, he became more comfortable, dancing and rapping along to the down south music blasting through the speakers. He was also a great hype man. Every pretty girl who walked by, he pulled them to the side, pointed at me, and said, "Did you see how my brother, Tootie, put on for the state of Georgia tonight?"

I lost count of how many autographs and selfies I took with fans because of him. With the amount of alcohol consumed, I wouldn't have remembered the number if I wanted to. I told myself after the shots I'd had on my recruiting visit that I wouldn't drink anymore.

Clearly, that didn't last. And like I said, I just wanted to show my big brother a good time. I still looked up to him. There were no worries when he was around. So, without hesitation, we both threw them back throughout the night.

13 IT WASN'T WORTH IT

I SHOWED OUT AGAIN FOR the people who thought I was a one-hit wonder. I followed up a four-touchdown first half game with another two touchdowns and 176 rushing yard performance against Auburn. That's six touchdowns in six quarters, but who's counting? I made it clear I was here to stay, and if they hadn't taken notice of me yet, maybe now was the time they should. I was Michael last week, but this week, Tootie caught on like wildfire. In fact, by the fourth quarter, the student section took it back to high school when they all shouted, "TOOTIE, TOOTIE" after I put the game away with my last touchdown. If I kept putting up those types of numbers, I'd likely make an All-American team.

My dad had been calling me every day since the Auburn game to tell me how I was not as good as my numbers suggested. I knew exactly what he was doing—talking down my game in fear of me getting ahead of myself. I'd been used to him doing that my entire life, but now my dad's criticism was easier to reject and push to the side when there were instructors and students on campus telling me how well I'd been playing. The adoration from thousands of people recognizing my skills outweighed what seemed like the one person who did not.

As for school, the past week was okay. After realizing from my first science exam that I could get a B by only studying for a couple of hours, it came back to bite me. Just the past week alone I'd received a C- on a math exam, and a D on a psychology exam. I just had to tighten up, then I'd be right back on track.

This coming Saturday we were set to face an Alabama team that was currently number one in the nation. There was no time to relax. It felt like I got a New York minute to celebrate before quickly needing to switch my focus in preparation for the next opponent. Our tenacious schedule reminded me of playing a video game where each level you surpassed, the game became tougher and tougher.

To kill time before psychology class, I ate lunch with a homesick Marcus. While I'd been playing lights out for the past two weeks, Marcus had been benched due to what the coaches called poor performance. I wouldn't go as far as saying his play was poor. Opposing teams targeted him because he was a freshman, and he just so happened to catch some unlucky breaks out on the field.

"I'm at the point where I'm ready to go to Coach Stuart's office and ask for a release from my scholarship and transfer elsewhere, Tootie," he said. "I didn't come here to sit the bench. I can be spending this time with my son back home in South Carolina."

"I was in the same boat, Marcus. But these things have a way of playing themselves out. I know this may sound cliché, but be patient, bro. You are, hands down, the best athlete on the team. And to be totally honest, how would it look if you went back home? I bet everyone from Charleston looks up to you. I bet everyone is rooting for you. You can't go back; you have to ride this wave to the end. Like it or not, you have the whole city on your back."

His face relaxed slightly. "Man, you are right. I do have a lot of people counting on me, and I have never quit before. I'm just in a dark space right now. I've never experienced getting moved to the sideline before. How did you handle your frustration when the coaches decided to go with Dominque to start the season?"

As I was about to answer, I got a call from Sophia. "Hold on real quick," I said to Marcus.

"Hey, baby," I greeted.

"I'm done with you, Tootie. I'm done with you!" she screamed.

I held up a finger to Marcus and quickly excused myself for some privacy.

What have I done to her? I tried my hardest to think back of any wrongdoings, but I was drawing a blank.

"Sophia, what are you talking about?"

"You know out of all the years I have known you, you have never given me a reason not to trust you—until now," she said through tears.

"Sophia, I don't get it. Why are you crying, and what have I done to make you this upset?"

"What have you done? I guess you haven't been on the internet, huh?" Her tone switched from hurt to anger. "As a matter of fact, I will text you the pictures."

"Hello? Sophia, Sophia!" I screamed, trying to stop her from hanging up in my ear, but I was too late. Seconds later, I received a string of pictures from her through text messages. The first photo was of me with my arm around another female. I quickly downplayed it as me taking a casual photo with a fan. *What's the big deal, and why is she making a fuss over this?*

As I scrolled up with my thumb, my stomach dropped. There were so many photos of me with different girls. Some of them were kissing on me, and others were doing worse. I could only imagine how Sophia felt when she saw them.

I quickly called her to apologize, but she ignored it. I tried several more times—still no answer. Sophia's dad left their family to start another one when she was in middle school. She made it clear before we started dating that she didn't trust easily. I always knew if I betrayed her, it would be the end of our relationship.

As crazy as this may sound, I didn't remember taking some of the photos. Like a detective, I went through each one carefully, analyzing everything from who was in the picture to what was in the background. And then my first clue hit me like a punch to the gut. I zoomed in and caught a glimpse of a smiling Shawn. The only time I was with Shawn was the weekend he came down to see my record-breaking performance against Tennessee. I was so stuck on making sure he had a good time that I consumed too much alcohol and lost control of my actions.

I dialed his number immediately. "Yo, Shawn. The whole night you were here, all you did was egg me on and pass me drinks. And because of that, I made a fool of myself and possibly lost Sophia."

"Man, slow down. Where is all this coming from?" he said.

"Like I said, man, you didn't try to stop my behavior like a real big brother would, you just went along with it."

"So what are you trying to say?"

"I said what I had to say. I just don't want to be the big brother when I already have one."

"I get what you're saying, but I didn't make you drink. I didn't make you do the things you did. So don't put that on me, little brother. Take some ownership. And how does Sophia know what went on, anyway?"

"Someone posted photos on social media." I replied.

"What were you doing in the pictures?"

"I wasn't doing anything, but the girls in the pics was kissing all over me."

"Sheesh! I guess Pops was right. People really know who you are now," he said. "Look, just tell Sophia you drank too much and allowed girls to get a little too close. Tell her nothing else happened, and in about a week or two, all will be forgotten."

"Yeah, thanks. That crap ain't gonna fly," I said sarcastically as I hung up the phone.

Psychology class could wait. My main objective was to get Sophia on the phone and try my best to smooth things over. *Even if I did get her on the phone, what could I possibly say?* I could tell her that the photos were photoshopped. *Yeah, right, she's far too intelligent to believe something like that.*

As psychology class went on without me, I sat by myself outside on a bench. I couldn't care less if Coach White or any of the other coaches were doing class checks. My mind was convoluted. All because of one stupid mistake, the future all of a sudden looked blurry and uncertain. Just yesterday I was thinking how Sophia and I were going to be the "it couple" after college. She was going to be a prestigious lawyer, and I was going to be Super Bowl-winning running back for the Dallas Cowboys. Man, I couldn't believe how badly I'd messed up. I even stooped so low as to put my mistakes on Shawn.

After stepping on the practice field, it felt like magic was hypnotizing my brain to not think about Sophia anymore. The football field had always been my sanctuary. Once on it, the outside world didn't exist. Maybe it was because the nature of the game, at least that's what my dad always told me. He would say, *"Football is 85 percent mental and 15 percent physical."* The moment you let personal issues onto the field is the moment you perform at your worst.

Practice was such a stress reliever. Being able to bang heads and fly around the field with my teammates brought me comfort. Even a couple hours after it had ended, I found myself in a reasonably good mood—until Sophia finally returned my phone call. As calm as one could be, she said, "I should've seen this coming. I've never been so hurt in my life. I was devastated when my father left, but this probably hurts even more. I don't care about the stories behind the photos, spare me the details. I just called to tell you how betrayed I feel."

"Let me explain, Sophia. I—"

"Umm, no, Michael. There is nothing you can say. I'm moving on with my life, and I suggest you do, too."

"What?"

"You always said you didn't want to be a player like your dad, but look at you."

"I'm not like him."

"Yes, you are."

"No, I'm not."

"There's no need to go back and forth here unless you can undo what you did in those pictures."

"You didn't see me do anything in those pics. Yeah, I let some girls get close and I'm sorry for that, but that's a far as it went." Shawn's advice was my last chance to save face.

"So, you're just going to lie to me like that, huh?"

"I'm not lying."

"I saw the caption one of the girls put under the pic. I know more happened that night."

"What caption?"

127

"Look, you know what you did, and to make it worse, you can't even own up to it. Just be honest about it, Tootie."

I couldn't continue to lie to her like that. I just couldn't. I mean, I loved her too much to keep up with this.

"Okay, Sophia, I messed up. I didn't mean for it to go that far."

"I knew it. I've held you down since the ninth grade. And now that you think you're big time, you go and cheat on me. I'm done with you, have a nice life."

And just like that, our four-year relationship was gone. My heart was in pieces. I couldn't explain how I was feeling. It was like falling from a thousand-foot cliff and bracing for rock bottom. I'd always avoided relationship problems, mainly because she was my first and only girlfriend.

To cope, I told myself that there was no use getting sad over females. I had to stay strong. There were plenty of girls out there. But, the tough guy act only lasted five minutes, and I was back to feeling hopeless again. I'd lost big football games before and been sad about it, but the current feeling I had did not compare.

Not knowing what to do, I called my dad and mustered up enough humility to tell him that Sophia and I split up, then I broke down over the phone.

"Son, it happens," he said. "What you need to do is focus on school and football."

That's all he has to say? During times like these, I missed my mom the most. She'd know exactly what to say if she were here. You'd think my dad would have some soothing words of encouragement after losing my mother, but apparently not. I'm sure people gave him soothing words after she passed away. To be respectful, I simply said, "Yes, sir. I have to get ready for bed. I'll call you later this week."

After I hung up the phone, I just lay in bed and stared at the ceiling. I could feel my heart growing colder by the minute.

Why does life have to be so hard? I wondered.

14 FAME CAN BE A DRUG

OVER THE LAST SEVERAL WEEKS, I could feel myself becoming a different person, an angrier, careless person with an ego of ten men. Truthfully, it made me a better football player, but worse in everything else. My motivation to score touchdowns and rush for over 140 yards per game was not to win. I was motivated for the cameras to be pointed at me and news articles to be written. In part, this was how I dealt with the dark cloud hovering over me from losing the woman of my dreams. I yearned for the attention of every girl on campus. I hated what I was turning into, but at the same time, I couldn't stop it.

When I talked to friends and family back home, they would say things like, "You are living the dream," or "I wish I was like you and decided to go to college and play ball." Little did they know, my stress and frustration had hit an all-time high. Of course, there was the Sophia thing, but on top of that, there was all this added pressure now.

There was pressure from coaches to give all we had in our final stretch of the season. We were in a three-way tie to see who would play for the conference championship, and our coaching staff had been pushing us to the limit. And with the season I'd had, there were extra media obligations. News outlets from all over the country were calling for interviews. Not only was I getting attention from the media, but I'd been the life of the party almost every night. From clubs, to house, fraternity, and sorority parties, you could count on Tootie being there. One place you could not count on me to be at was class the next morning. Something had to give with all that was going on, and I chose to sacrifice academics.

At a minimum, I skipped two classes out of the week to sleep. And when I did decide to go, I would walk around campus with a hoodie over my head like a sleep-walking zombie. So, I figured if I was going to sleep in class, I might as well stay in bed.

I continued this routine until Terrell showed up in my dorm room.

"Tootie, you are on the verge of losing everything you worked hard for. We haven't had a talented running back like you in a while," he said. "Marcus told me you were going through a relationship thing or whatever, but going out drinking and partying every night ain't the way to handle it, man. You're lucky the coaches haven't caught wind of any of this."

"Dang, Marcus is just going to snitch on me like that?" I let out a deep sigh. "Man, you are right. I gotta snap out of this funk."

"I've seen the most talented get bounced up out of here, man. I mean guys who could have been all-world. Trust me, you got to get out of this 'it's all about me' mood you're in. What you do affects the team, and me as well. Believe it or not, you play a vital role in my draft stock. How many classes have you been skipping, anyway?" Terrell asked.

"I've lost count at this point," I answered. "I will go and talk to each of my instructors and get everything squared away."

"Yeah, man, I would encourage you to do that. Do you remember me telling you that everything is not what it appears to be on your recruiting visit?"

"Yeah, I do."

"People will give their right leg to be in our shoes until they are in our shoes," Terrell said with the most serious face I've ever seen. "On the other hand, we are blessed to be where we are and wouldn't trade it for anything. But just because we're here doesn't mean we don't go through trials. Trials come with being the man on campus. We have to grow up quicker than everybody else so we can handle all of this. I know on your visit you couldn't wait to leave home and experience this different world. Now that you're in it, you see everything is not as easy as it is standing on the other side. Now get up out of your bed and handle your issues like a grown man."

Terrell shot it to me straight, as only a natural-born leader could. I was grateful. He certainly didn't have to come to my dorm room and check on me.

With newfound motivation, I wasted no time getting dressed so I could visit my psychology instructor. I was hoping that he'd give me a break and let me make up some missed assignments.

I knocked on Professor Gray's office door. He was in the middle of a phone conversation but signaled for me to take a seat in a chair across from his desk. I avoided staring at him while he was talking by exploring the room. His office was neatly organized, filled with books, family portraits, and plaques hanging on walls from the various awards he'd been honored with. I turned 180 degrees to quickly see what was on the wall behind me. As I was turning back to face Instructor Gray, I did a double take when I noticed a jersey in a frame hanging high on the wall. It was a #38 University of Georgia football jersey with *Gray* printed in white across the back. *Was Instructor Gray one of us? Surely he'd give me a break, right?* He of all people should understand firsthand what a student-athlete has to endure.

After he hung up the phone, I said, "I didn't know you played here back in the day."

"Yeah, that frame serves as a reminder."

"A reminder of what?" I asked.

"Football doesn't define me. It was just a small part of me that lasted only a couple years. What does define me is what's in here." He pointed to his temple.

This just went far left, I thought to myself.

"If you would've never entered my office, you'd never know that I played college football. I never wanted to be one of those old guys who sat around drinking beers, saying, 'In my heyday, this is what I did on the field.' I experienced a lot in during my glory days, but football is the last topic I ever bring up," he said. "But, I'm sure you didn't come in here to hear me go on a tangent.... So, I haven't seen you around lately. What brings you to my office?"

"Well, I haven't been myself lately. I've been going through some personal issues. That's the reason I've missed the last several classes, including quizzes and exams. I'm here to ask you if there's something I can do to make up missed assignments."

"You haven't been sick. I know that because of the terrific season you have been having thus far. So, did a loved one pass away or something?" Instructor Gray asked.

"No, no one has died or anything, sir, just been dealing with some stuff," I answered.

"I don't get it, Michael. If you can go out there on Saturdays and play a football game. A game, I repeat, and not consider how important your education is, then that shows me where your priorities lie. I'd be doing you a huge disservice in allowing you to make up assignments. I wouldn't allow it for other students, so I can't show you preferential treatment. You may not understand this now, but there's a valuable lesson that I hope will come out of this one day."

"Thanks for nothing," I said before storming out.

The man acts like I was asking for a handout or something. He was probably a horrible football player. I bet he never saw the field. I'm sure that's the reason why he doesn't bring it up.

Still feeling concerned about my grades, I decided to meet with Mr. Hernandez, my academic advisor.

"Hello, Tootie! Congrats to you on a stellar freshman season so far. It's a surprise to see you," Mr. Hernandez greeted. "You haven't been by here to see me since the beginning of the semester. How is everything going?"

"I've had better days, Mr. Hernandez. I'm concerned about my grades and want to seek your advice on how I can finish the semester strong."

"What do you mean you're concerned? You have been a constant at study hall throughout the semester, at least according to my records."

"Yeah, about that…. I went to study hall to sign in and snuck out immediately afterwards."

"Tootie," he said, disappointed.

"I know, I know."

"Let me pull up your records so we can find out," he said. "You started off strong in most of your courses, but have since fallen off a cliff. But, I think you still have a chance of at least maintaining a 2.0 GPA if you buckle down this last month of the semester. Have you talked to any of your instructors? Most of the instructors here are willing to help."

"Yes, sir. I went to Instructor's Grays office earlier and he basically said beat it."

"He's known to be tough on athletes. But no worries, he owes me a favor. I will talk to him tomorrow and see what we can do. But, this is your one freebie. Next time, you need to stay on top of your studies, or come and see much earlier."

"Thank you, sir," I said before exiting his office.

The next morning, I made a rare appearance at my 8:00 a.m. science class. Surprisingly, my seat next to Jennifer wasn't filled with cobwebs.

"You become this big football star and start missing classes, huh?" Jennifer said. "Well, your timing is perfect. We have an exam today."

"Are you serious?" I asked.

"As serious as a heart attack."

The joke was on me. If I didn't pass this test, I'd run the risk of falling below a 2.0 and being placed on academic probation next semester, making me ineligible to play if we went to a January bowl game.

The same feeling I'd get before a big game was the same feeling I had now. I was as nervous as a fly trapped in a bug zapper. This was sure to be the death of me. I only had a couple options at this point: I could fake a stomach virus and hope the instructor would let me take the test after I had a chance to study, or I could go in blind and pray I chose the right answers. Or…I could just copy off of Jennifer's exam. I knew for sure she'd studied, and just like the previous exam, I bet she'd leave her test uncovered, inviting me to copy her answers.

I hated to double back on my morals, but I needed to do what was best for me in this instance. When I got my test, I checked Jennifer's to ensure we had the same version. I'd hate to cheat and lose it all by copying the wrong answers. After confirming we did, I pretended to read each question while simultaneously copying her answers. Cheating was as just as stressful as studying. I had to make sure no one was watching me, while still guaranteeing I was copying her answers correctly.

After Jennifer completed the test and turned it in, I stayed for an extra ten minutes—just to make sure no one was on to me. After determining I was in the clear, I got up and turned my exam in without a bit of worry.

Whew, I just successfully lived to see another day.

15 FINISH STRONG. TOOTIE

"I HOPE AND PRAY THAT every person in this room lives to see ninety years old, I really do. Over the next several decades, you all will experience some amazing things. But, I can promise you this, when you get to your ninetieth birthday, you will always remember what you are about to do over these next sixty minutes. If you go out there and leave it all on the field, these next sixty minutes will be one of the proudest moments of your life," Coach Stuart said before the conference championship game in Atlanta, Georgia.

Coach Stuart's words made me pause for a moment and think about how far I'd come since arriving in Athens six months ago. My mind quickly flashed through some of my highest and lowest points—Shawn and Dad dropping me off, the grind of practicing throughout the summer in the sweltering Georgia heat, ultimately becoming the start-ing running back, experiencing the joy of scoring my first collegiate touchdown in front of 100,000 people, surviv-ing a breakup and almost losing my mind in the college party scene, and, eventually, figuring out a way to manage school and instant notoriety. They say what doesn't kill you makes you stronger, and after all that I'd been through in just one semester, I was stronger than ever.

Our team knew what was at stake here. With two losses on our record, it was a long shot to make it to the national championship. But with a win in tonight's con-ference championship game against the ferocious Ala-bama team, who knew where the chips will fall. Depending on the results of other games being played, we could very well position ourselves with a win to compete for a national title.

Once our inspired ball club took the field, it didn't take long for us to start clicking. After an early intercep-tion by Marcus, I was quickly set up to rush for my 14th touchdown of the year on our first offensive possession. After scoring, I jogged to the sideline and found Marcus to give him a big a hug.

"Bro, I never got a chance to say thanks for looking out for me, if you didn't tell Terrell how I was slipping, who knows where I would be," I said during our embrace.

"Man, that's what brothers are for," he said, then ran back on the field for defense.

Marcus and I had gotten tight since meeting each other on report day back in the summer. I'd always heard some of your best friends in the world would be made in college, but now I wholeheartedly believed it. We were both stuck in freshman ruts, but were able to help each other through some difficult times. Needless to say, Marcus regained his starting spot and had been playing like a real baller ever since.

We eventually won the game against Alabama 28–14, avenging our earlier loss and securing our first conference championship in almost fifteen years. Confetti dropped from the sky like raindrops—a celebration reminiscent of the late-night parties I'd attended around campus. Coach was right; I'd remember this moment for as long as I'd live.

We headed to the locker room, and as usual, my phone was buzzing off the hook with congratulatory messages from family and friends. But a fairly more mature me didn't let the *you're the man,* or, *you're a future first-round pick* messages get to my head as it had earlier in the season. When our media relations representative came to tell me I'd been requested for interviews, I decided to bring our entire offensive line to field questions. These guys were the reason we'd had a successful season, and rarely did they get a chance to talk to the media.

When one reporter asked why I brought my bodyguards, I answered by saying, "I don't have much to say today. I would much rather have you guys ask our offensive line questions, because they are the real reason for our team's success."

I left the press conference and greeted Dad and Shawn on the field.

"I am so proud of you, son," Dad said in the happiest tone I'd ever heard.

Everything was on the up and up for me. It was good to take a step back for a second and take in the beauty of being a college athlete. It was also good to see confirmation of making the correct choice in where to attend. I apologized to Instructor Gray for the way I behaved in his office, and Mr. Hernandez worked it out with him last week; I was in the process of making up missed assignments. My other instructors allowed me to do the same. Who knows, I might land a 2.5 GPA by the time the semester ends. I knew I didn't deserve it, but I was grateful for the second chance. And seeing how happy Dad was brought everything else full circle.

The next day, after arriving back in Athens, we met at the football facility to watch the selection show. The selection show would decide our fate as we hoped to be chosen as one of four teams to compete in January's college football playoffs. We had no idea what the committee was going to decide. All we knew was we beat an undefeated Alabama team by 14 points, and we were deserving of the opportunity.

I sat in my normal seat in the third row, anxiously watching the giant projector just like everybody else in the room. Before I knew what was coming, a giant Georgia football helmet popped on the screen to signify we were in. Our meeting room erupted with cheers, fist pumps, and high fives. We had a date against Penn State on New Year's Day in Pasadena, California. Life didn't get much better.

I quickly pulled out my phone to Facetime my dad and share the excitement.

"My flight and hotel are in the process of being booked," he said proudly.

Coach Stuart gave the team the following week off from all football-related activities—aside from weightlift-ing—to prepare for final exams. I didn't have a worry in the world. I wasn't even letting the pressure of finals get to me.

While in the players' lounge playing video games the next evening, I received a call from Coach Stuart to come into his office. I hadn't talked to Coach Stuart over the phone since the recruiting process in high school. The only thing I could think of was him personally wanting to tell me I'd been chosen as the conference player of the year or something. I surely didn't think I'd done anything wrong. It'd been a couple of weeks since I skipped a class or was out partying late.

When I got to Coach Stuart's office, Coach White and Coach Smith were there waiting for me. Along with the three coaches, there was also my science instructor. I knew instantly this wasn't going to go well. Coach Stuart told me to have a seat.

"Do you know why I've called you into my office, Tootie? Look around at who is in here and think before you answer."

Maybe he wants to discuss the classes I missed. Certainly, he couldn't accuse me of cheating with no proof. Unless Jennifer snitched on me, but she didn't know I was copying her test, and that exam was two weeks ago. I even took the liberty of changing answers so we wouldn't end up with the exact score.

"I'm not sure, Coach Stuart."

"That is the wrong answer, Tootie. So, I'll ask it a better way. Do you know why Instructor Roberts and your coaches are in here? I'll give you a hint: it's not football-related," Coach Stuart said.

"Coach, I really don't know. You're asking me questions like you think I've done something. I missed a couple of classes, but other than that, I don't know why I'm here."

"Instructor Roberts came to me and said there has been an honor code violation involving exams," Coach Stuart explained. "A violation of the honor code can result in expulsion from the university. Instead of Instructor Roberts taking this matter to the school board, he approached me so we could resolve it internally. But, to fix this matter, I need honesty and transparency. I'm not asking as your coach anymore, I'm asking man to man. Did you cheat on an exam?"

The guilt was bursting out of my eyelids in the form of tears. I wasn't sure how they knew I'd cheated, but they got me.

"Yes, sir."

"Michael, you weren't in any of my classes for three weeks. It's almost impossible to get a 96 on one of my exams without attending class. I let you make up assignments, and you didn't come close to obtaining a 96. How did you manage to get a high score on a test you weren't in class for, but you barely received a 70 on an exam you were in class for? In the future, if you are having issues, come to me. I take the school's honor code seriously. Even if you need help, come to me, this is why I teach. This time I will not report this matter like we are required, but I will have to fail you," Instructor Roberts said.

"Thank you, Instructor Roberts," I said.

He left the office shortly after that.

I began to apologize to my coaches. "I promise this was the first time I've ever cheated on anything in my life. Sorry I lied, I just...."

"Tootie, you are one of the best players on this team, and whether you are a freshman or not, your teammates look up to you. You could've put this team in serious jeopardy. Why apologize afterward if you knew you were lying beforehand. What are my four rules?"

"Respect women, don't lie, no drugs, and no guns," I answered.

"Exactly, if all I cared about were football games, then I wouldn't be a good coach. I care more about integrity, and in this case, you didn't show any."

I didn't say another word. What could I say? I'd lied to him, and to Coach Stuart—that was the ultimate sign of disrespect. I was sure he was going to make me run like crazy during our next practice.

"I swear, if the other hundred kids on this team weren't depending on you, I would suspend your butt right now," Coach Stuart said angrily. "Get out of my office. I'm so disappointed in you."

I knew I shouldn't have cheated. I was lucky it didn't cost me big time. I didn't return to the players' lounge to play any more video games. Instead, I went to Mr. Hernandez's office to get clarification on Instructor Roberts saying he was failing me. Did he mean he was going to give me a zero on the exam, or was he going to fail me for the semester? I was so caught up in the relief of not getting expelled that I didn't think to ask. If he failed me for the semester, I was sure I'd be academically ineligible. I'd be placed on probation and unable to play in our playoff game.

I explained everything to Mr. Hernandez and didn't leave anything unsaid. I talked about Sophia and my struggles. And, of course, he scolded me for not coming to him or any of the coaches earlier. In hindsight, I wished I had. It was so easy for me to get caught up in the limelight instead of dealing with my problems head-on. Even afterward, I thought none of my mess was going to come back and bite me. I still had hope, but Mr. Hernandez told me to wait a couple of days and he would talk to my instructor and coaches to see what was going on.

This must've been the same feeling my brother had before he was sentenced to jail. I was petrified. As the next couple days passed, I took my final exams and waited. Two days after my last exam, Mr. Hernandez called me to his office and relayed the news.

"Tootie, you finished the semester with a 1.8 GPA. Because you admitted to cheating, the only course of action for Instructor Roberts to take besides reporting academic dishonesty was to fail you."

"So what does this mean?" I asked, as if I didn't already know. Sometimes it's just better to hear it out of someone else's mouth.

"You will be placed on academic probation until you achieve higher than a 2.0 next semester," Mr. Hernandez replied.

It was as if someone reached into my heart and smashed it with a hammer repeatedly. I let down the entire community. *What will my dad say? The people back home in Virginia? What will my teammates think of me now?* I was sure our chances of winning a championship were slim to none now.

"Sorry, Tootie. I will let the coaches know."

I went to my dorm and cried myself to sleep. I didn't call my dad or say anything to anyone. I convinced myself I was in a nightmare, and when I woke up, I'd realize that. But instead, I woke up, checked the internet, and the headlines read: "Standout Georgia Bulldogs Freshman Running Back, Tootie Mayberry, Suspended For College Football Playoffs."

To be continued....

About the Author

Eugene D. Holloman is a former 2x all-conference running back at James Madison University. Growing up he had aspirations of playing professional football after college, but after two significant knee surgeries before his senior year, his plans were derailed. After graduating with a degree and pursuing a major simple enough to keep him eligible but that honestly disinterested him, Eugene quickly regretted not taking school more seriously. While some of his college buddies were off to corporate careers or entrepreneurship, Eugene spent the next four years in his parents' home discovering his passions and what career path he wanted to pursue. Eugene enrolled in a master's program to pursue his MBA while working as an elementary school tutor and sales rep for a high-end suit retailer. While not making enough money to pay for school, he eventually landed an entry-level job at a Fortune 500 healthcare company. Soon thereafter, he applied and was hired to the company's leadership development program.

Eugene is now a corporate compliance manager for the same company and is currently pursuing his doctoral degree at Regent University. He credits Regent University for helping him discover his passion for writing within just his first couple of semesters of attendance. While writing numerous research papers on leadership, Eugene decided to write his first fictional novel: *The Athlete-Student: Freshman Year*. His goal is to reach as many student-athletes and youth as possible in hopes that this story will benefit them, as Eugene believes having such an inspiring read would have been highly impactful when he was in high school.

Follow Eugene:

Facebook: https://www.facebook.com/eugene.holloman

Instagram: https://www.instagram.com/geneduke14/

Twitter: https://twitter.com/geneduke14

Pinterest: https://www.pinterest.com/eugeneholloman/

LinkedIn: https://www.linkedin.com/in/eugene-holloman-13415b65/